DOUBLE PLAY
ROOKIE

by the author of
INSIDE TACKLE • HOLD THAT LINE
FIGHTING COACH • BLOCK THAT KICK

Joe Archibald

DOUBLE PLAY
ROOKIE

Macrae Smith Company
PHILADELPHIA

jAr25d

U. S.918371

TO ALL FUTURE BIG LEAGUERS,
reminding them that there is a fifth base on a baseball diamond, reached only by those who consider their greatest reward a feeling of satisfaction for having played the game. In the thrilling cry of "PLAY BALL!" there is the pure ring of democracy.

DOUBLE PLAY ROOKIE

CHAPTER 1

ALL RIGHT, LEFTY!" CALLED JOHNNY GRAMNER, PLAY-ing the keystone sack for the North Side Barons. "You can get this big guy!" He stopped quickly, picked up a pebble and tossed it to the skin of the infield. The Barons, one of Bridge City's leading semipro ball clubs, had come into the last half of the eighth with a two-run lead, but Lefty Poole had suddenly lost his control and now the Grays had the bases loaded and nobody out.

Lefty stepped off the rubber, making the hitter wait. He went to the rosin bag and dried his pitching hand. Johnny straightened up, turned, and looked at the outfielders. He waved Eddie Nelson deeper in left. Johnny had been playing ball ever since he'd been big enough to keep a regulation-size glove on his left hand, and his idol was Nellie Fox of the White Sox. He was just over eighteen, dark-haired and dark-eyed, and stood five feet nine in his stocking feet. He had barely a trace of a lantern jaw that accounted for the aggressiveness he showed on the diamond, but his greatest asset was a pair of big hands. In two years of semipro ball his fielding had been close to perfect, and he'd always hit well over .300.

"Don't let him see the fast one," Johnny chirped as Lefty toed the rubber again. The man at the plate had

9

big shoulders and a stance patterned after the great Musial's.

Lefty just missed the corner with a fast one, then threw one into the dirt that the Baron catcher had to smother with his body. The Sunday afternoon crowd of nearly a thousand started clapping. Johnny called time and ran in to steady Lefty. "Just get it over, Lefty. Make him hit it on the ground."

His infield set again, Lefty pumped twice and fired his fast one. The batter swung and smashed it toward Allie Macri at short. Allie dug it out and scooped it over to Johnny Gramner, racing to cover the middle sack. Johnny took the ball, leaped out of range of the spikes of the runner trying to take him out, and fired it to Stretch Kelly at first for the double play. A run came over, and a Gray was waiting to be picked up at third.

"That's all they get," Johnny called out. "Throw that rock, Lefty!"

The Baron southpaw bent forward to get the catcher's sign, but shook it off. Then he nodded and threw without a windup. The batter swung and fouled it over the stands. Lefty put too much on his next pitch and it went wide of the plate, out of the catcher's reach, and the tying run came in when the ball rolled all the way to the backstop. Johnny Gramner slammed his glove down. "You're beating yourself, Lefty!" he yelled.

The Baron pitcher got the next man on a high pop just outside third base, and the Grays took the field. Johnny Gramner was still a little stormy when he reached the Baron bench. Jumbo Mace, the catcher, said, "So they tied us. We still got out of that inning lucky."

"We could lose," Johnny snapped.

"Why, sure." Jumbo grinned. "We've lost before."

10

They watched Chick Tamicci take the count all the way to three and two against the Gray right-hander, then pop weakly to the first baseman. Johnny picked up a bat and walked out to hit; the Baron sympathizers begged him to get hold of one. So far he had been held to a scratch single. He looked at the redhead on the mound and hoped the man would throw his curve. The first one came in high and fast for a ball. He took the next one around the knees for a called strike and stepped out and banged dirt off his spikes.

The Gray shortstop yelled, "Tie him in a knot, Mitch!"

The curve came in, not too fast, and hung. Johnny timed it right, got the good wood on the ball, and drove it up the wide alley between the Grays' right fielder and center fielder. The ball hit the fence and bounced back. As Johnny rounded second he heard the warning yell from the third-base coach and guessed the relay in was going to be close. Ten feet from the bag he hit the dirt, saw the ball hit the third baseman's glove, and slid around the tag in a cloud of dust. The umpire called him safe. He got up, banging the dirt from his pants and grinning at Pat Brophy, the manager and third-base coach.

"Grandstand," Pat yelled at him. "I held you up!"

"You can't score from second on a sacrifice fly," Johnny told him.

A few moments later he was running home after Jumbo Mace had banged a long fly to deep left, and again the Barons were ahead, 6–5. The Baron left fielder struck out, and Lefty Poole strode to the mound.

The Grays' catcher, a power hitter, led off. He slammed Lefty's first pitch past the mound and to all appearances had a hit. But Johnny raced over, back-

11

handed the smash near the keystone sack, and threw to first off balance. Stretch Kelly dug it out of the dirt a second ahead of the runner, and the fans gasped. Johnny walked back to his position, wondering why things could not happen the way they did in books. Why couldn't a scout from the majors be in those stands?

Lefty Poole, after his second baseman's save, felt bigger and stronger than when he'd started. He struck out the Grays' third baseman with four pitched balls and got a pinch hitter to foul out to Jumbo Mace, winding up the ball game. The Barons ran off, chattering like chipmunks. Johnny put his arm around Lefty. "Only seven hits. You were great, Lefty!"

"You saved me twice," the pitcher said.

Johnny looked at the dispersing crowd. "At fifty cents a head," he said, "we ought to get maybe—"

"Afraid of gettin' shortchanged, Johnny?" Jumbo Mace laughed.

"Maybe I play this game to get a sun tan," the second sacker said.

"A lot of fun in it," Lefty Poole said. "You take it too seriously, Johnny."

"Maybe I don't want to drive a truck all my life."

"Look," Jumbo Mace said, tucking his chest protector under his arm, "only one in a million gets to the big leagues."

"I'm one of 'em," Johnny told him, and then he saw Pat Brophy motioning to him near the exit gate. With Pat was a tall man wearing a light summer suit and a chocolate-colored straw hat with a white band. His face was that of one who spends most of his time outdoors, squinting into the sun.

"Johnny," Pat said, "meet Dan Kelso. He was in the

12

stands watching you. Ten years ago he played with the Minneapolis Blues."

Kelso held out his hand. "Nice to meet you, Gramner, in more ways than one. You make the double play very good."

"Thanks," Johnny said, his blood running faster. "You a scout from the big leagues?"

"Not so fast." Dan Kelso grinned. "Let's creep a little before we walk. My car's out there. I could drive you home and we could have a talk."

"Sure." Johnny felt embarrassed. "It isn't a ritzy neighborhood where I live, though." He walked off with Kelso and called back to the other Barons, "See you later, bushers!"

In Kelso's big car Johnny sank deep into the cushions and told himself he would have a car like this some day. "Drive straight across town," he directed. "Then downtown to West Lancey. I live two blocks from the river. You mind walking up five flights?"

Dan Kelso, when he swung into Johnny's street, had to admit he had never seen a more dingy row of tenement houses. He'd read about this part of Bridge City in out-of-town newspapers. The kids brought up here, he thought—well, the old cliché fitted them: they had two strikes called against them the day they were born.

"Pretty crumby," Johnny said. "I was born here."

Kelso said, "You have a home, Johnny."

"Such as it is, Mr. Kelso."

"Remember one thing, Johnny Gramner," Kelso said quietly. "Babe Ruth never had a home."

"Yeah," Johnny said, "that's right. That's the tenement I live in, over by that pile of garbage cans. I'd lock the car, Mr. Kelso."

"As bad as that?"

Johnny nodded. "I ought t' know. I learned the hard way."

Dan Kelso looked around him as he parked the sedan. Here was insecurity and uncertainty, the heritage of the poor. He followed Johnny into a dim hallway full of stale and unpleasant smells, and then up five flights of dingy stairs.

When they reached the sixth-floor landing, the door of a flat flew open and a boy with a mop of sandy hair came running out. He stopped in his tracks when he saw Dan Kelso.

"Sure, we won, Ricky," Johnny said. "Six to five. This is my kid brother, Mr. Kelso."

"Glad to know you, Ricky," Kelso said, and then followed Johnny into the Gramner flat. It wasn't much. The plaster was cracked, the old woodwork had been painted and repainted, and the linoleum on the floor was worn to the quick. The woman who looked at him critically was probably no older than Kelso, but she could have passed for ten years his senior. She seemed resigned to a grim acceptance of life, a woman enduring with proud obstinacy.

"Ma," Johnny said, "this is Mr. Kelso. I think he wants to give me a job playing ball."

"So?" She nodded to Dan Kelso. "Won't you sit down?"

Rick Gramner said excitedly, "Johnny, Mr. Sava gimme a job in the bowlin' alley. Settin' up pins after school."

"Nice goin', Rick," Johnny said.

"I don't know what we'd do around here without Al

Sava," Mrs. Gramner said. "He's the only one around this district who gives our kids a break."

"He must be O.K.," Dan Kelso said.

Johnny excused himself. "I'll get out of my uniform, Mr. Kelso, and be right back."

"Baseball is all he thinks about," Mrs. Gramner said. "He should get a steady job."

"Baseball can be a steady job," Kelso said. "There's a great future in it for a kid like Johnny."

Kelso perceived that Mrs. Gramner was not impressed. When Johnny came out of the bedroom, he immediately stated his business. "I'm manager of the Carlton Braves, a class C minor league club of the Ohio Valley League. We need a second baseman, and I know you can fill the bill. It's a step up, Johnny. Your foot is in the door. It isn't Pullman cars and swank hotels. It's busses and small commercial hotels and maybe boarding houses. You'll get sixty dollars every week and your keep."

Johnny's eyes grew bright. His mother said, "You want him so bad, Mr. Kelso, he should ask for more."

Johnny's lips tightened and he seemed to be thinking of something. "Yeah, Mr. Kelso, what about that?"

"I can't offer you any more. Maybe I can make a deal with the boss." Kelso studied the semipro player for a long moment. "Like a little extra as a bonus if you hit over three hundred. That won't be easy. I'll be honest with you. We have pitchers who have been in the big leagues. Making their last stop—"

"Sounds fair to me," Johnny broke in. "I can send Ma thirty every week. When do I sign?"

"Soon as we reach Carlton," Dan Kelso said. "Can you leave in the morning?"

"I'm ready now. I only have one suit to pack."

15

No mention had been made of Johnny and Rick's father. Kelso guessed they hadn't had one for quite some time. It was best, he decided, to make no inquiry.

"I'll call for you at nine in the morning, Johnny. We're opening a three-game series with the league-leaders day after tomorrow."

"I'll walk down with you, Mr. Kelso," Johnny said.

On the sidewalk a heavy-set man wearing loud sport clothes called to Johnny. He was fat-faced with an oily skin and a small black mustache. There was a small scar on his chin.

"Hi, Al," Johnny said. "This is Dan Kelso. He's hiring me to play in the minors. Say, about your sawbuck—I had to hurry home after the game today. You can collect it from Pat Brophy along with my share."

"Yeah, O.K." Sava nodded to Kelso. The Carlton manager looked at the beefy man, wondering if he had not met him somewhere before. He could forget a face or a name easily enough, but something about a man's gait always catalogued him.

"Great, Johnny, great," Al Sava said. "Keep in touch with me. Don't let the bushers push you around, and remember what I've told you." He eyed Kelso dubiously. "This kid knows the score, Kelso. I hope you'll pay him what he's worth."

"We'll be the judge of that, Sava," Dan Kelso told him. "Well, Johnny, be ready at nine in the morning." He got into the sedan and drove away. In the rearview mirror he saw Johnny and Al Sava walk down the street together. He must remember to ask Johnny what kind of a deal he had with the fat man.

Late the next afternoon Dan Kelso drew up in front of a brick building in the little city of Carlton, and

16

Johnny looked out at a big plate glass window that said *George C. Latham—Real Estate & Insurance*.

"Thought we'd have you sign up first thing," Dan said, "Latham's going out of town for a few days, and we might miss him."

"O.K. with me," the second baseman said. "Sure is a hick town."

On the way from Bridge City Kelso had had a chance to size up Johnny Gramner. The player admitted Sava had taken a cut out of his semipro earnings because the man had steered him to the Barons.

"It's business," Johnny had said. "Baseball is a business, right? No sentiment in it, no more than anything else. A man can be the best player in the majors. He runs against a fence, ruins himself for life. You have to get it in a hurry, Al said. He knew a guy once—"

Latham got up from the desk in the inner office when Kelso brought Johnny in. He was a middle-aged solid man with a ready smile, wearing a wrinkled cord suit. "So this is the new Charley Gehringer, Dan," he said, holding out his hand to Johnny.

"He's everything they said he was, George," Kelso said. "He might be the answer."

Latham sighed deeply and settled back in his chair. "I sure hope so, Dan. He like your terms?"

"I want another ten extra a week," Johnny said, "if I hit over three hundred. I want it in writing that I can be a free agent any time I want."

Dan Kelso's face clouded a little. Latham paused as he opened the drawer of his desk. "Quite a businessman for your age, Gramner," he said with a half smile. "I can't offer you a contract like that. I think somebody has been giving you poor advice." He slammed the drawer

17

shut. "Dan, we'll have to go along with Arkie Braun."

Kelso said, "All right, Johnny. We'll give you bus fare back to Bridge City. You can wait there until a better contract comes along."

Johnny Gramner looked a little deflated. "I—well, you can't blame me for trying, Mr. Latham. All right, I'll sign."

A few minutes later Kelso drove Johnny to the other side of town and put him up at a small family hotel run by one of the most rabid Carlton fans, Mrs. Grady. She was a stout little woman with sharp dark eyes, and knew the batting average of every ballplayer in the major leagues.

"If he hits under two eighty, Dan," Mrs. Grady said when she showed Johnny his room, "I'll throw him out."

Dan sat down and talked to Johnny for a few minutes. "You've got a lot to learn, kid. This isn't sand-lot ball, and you'll be playing with men who have been in big league parks. They're on their last legs, to be sure, but they've still got all they learned inside their heads. I'll help you all I can. If you can take criticism, I'll make a ballplayer out of you. If you can stand the jockeying of the other players, that is. They're masters at it, so don't get rabbit ears!"

"You learned to take it where I came from," Johnny said. "You dished it out, too, Mr. Kelso."

"One thing you have to remember. Keep your temper and don't ever use your fists," the manager said. "And forget what certain men have told you about this game of baseball. To you it is a business, you say. The fans call it a game, and it is a religion with most of them. And they pay your salary, don't ever forget it."

18

"Yeah," Johnny said. "Is there a movie in this one-horse town?"

"Get to bed early," Kelso spoke sharply. "We work out tomorrow afternoon. Most of our games are under the lights. It might take you a while to get used to night ball."

"I'll do all right," Johnny said.

Dan Kelso went out of the room and closed the door softly behind him. Mrs. Grady was waiting for him down the hall. "What do you think, sweetheart?" he asked her.

"He looks like a ballplayer," Mrs. Grady said, "except for one thing. He doesn't smile enough, Dan."

Kelso nodded. "I know what you mean."

CHAPTER 2

FARRINGTON PARK, HOME OF THE CARLTON BRAVES, was not far from the tracks of the Central Ohio railroad, a stereotyped, splinter-fenced plant with wooden seats badly in need of paint and with a roof over the reserved seats. It could accommodate two thousand fans.

Dan Kelso brought the new second baseman into the locker room at three o'clock the following afternoon and introduced him to the fifteen Carlton players, an assortment of inexperienced youths and veterans who had known better days. Some of them were already in uniform.

Johnny said, "Hi," and opened the door of the locker Kelso pointed out to him. A leathery-faced man with a sprinkling of gray at the temples asked, "When are you sending Arkie to the glue factory, Dan?"

"He bought himself a chicken farm," Kelso said. "He'll be on hand if we need him."

A short wiry man a little older than Johnny approached the new second baseman. "I'm Joey Olma, the shortstop, Gramner. We do business together. We stop a lot of hits now."

"I'll be tryin'." Johnny looked at the legs of a man standing a few feet away from him. They were covered with old scars. This was Irv Kevlow, the Braves third baseman, who Johnny learned later had played part of a season with the Cincinnati Reds.

The Carlton roster consisted of four infielders, five pitchers, two catchers and three outfielders, and a utility man. Pitchers sometimes had to be called in from the bull pen to play the outer garden. The word *Braves* on the suits had faded from black to a dirty gray and the stripe on the socks was nearer pink than red.

"We need hitting," Kelso said. "We'll work in the cage most of the afternoon." He looked at Johnny Gramner. His cap was too small. An old campaigner said, "It will fit in a couple of days, Dan."

"What was the idea of that crack?" Johnny snapped.

The other players looked at him. Some of them exchanged glances and grinned briefly. Kelso said, "Let's get out there."

Johnny, still stung, left the locker room. When he reached the dirt runway that led under the stands to the home team's dugout, a chunky man in a blue and red sport shirt got up off the bench and brashly looked

20

him up and down. Players nodded to the man and started ribbing him. Kelso said, "Johnny, this is Matt Yager, sports editor of the Carlton *Advertiser*."

"Glad to meetcha," Johnny said, and looked out at the sun-parched infield. Hard as a rock, he thought. There were bare patches in the outfield that was not too flat. He'd played on better ground in the city.

"Lots of luck, Gramner," Yager said. "We all need it. Dan, who starts tonight?"

"Haven't made up my mind, Matt. Maybe Mose Watson."

"Old Mose? He's been gettin' the lumps lately, Dan."

"And no support," Kelso reminded him.

"Hope you've plugged that hole." Yager turned to Johnny. "What did you hit on the sand lots, kid?"

"Three sixty-one."

"Hit seventy points below that here an' you stay," the writer said.

Kelso sent his hitters out and called on his top relief pitcher to throw. He sent them up in the order he used in the league games, Joey Olma leading off. The little Cuban sprayed a few short ones around, and then Fireman McBride threw some fast ones at Kelso's outfielder, Cy Sheckard. Cy rattled two of the offerings against the old fence in deep left and skied one to the infield. Matt Yager came in closer when Johnny Gramner was told to take his cuts.

The fireman looked at the fly shaggers and waved them in. The Carlton players laughed. The kid from Bridge City felt his ears burn, then he thought of Kelso's advice about rabbit ears and dug in. McBride threw him a high wide one and he swung and missed, nearly falling into the dirt.

21

"Watch for a good ball, Gramner," Kelso yelled.

The fireman threw a curve. Johnny grinned as he timed it right and slammed it far down the right-field line into the tacky bleachers. He kept swinging, hoping these wiseacres were getting an eyeful. When he'd driven two out of the park, Kelso called him out. "Save some for tonight, Johnny."

The rookie leaned against the cage and watched one of Kelso's cleanup hitters, Ox Janosky, drive two out of the park. He knew the fireman was grooving them for the big Carlton catcher. "What's he hitting?" he asked Flit Buhel, the Braves' left fielder.

"Three forty-three. He's kept us up in fourth place," Buhel replied. "Our only three-hundred hitter."

"Maybe," Johnny said.

Buhel eyed him for a moment, spat into the dirt.

Dan Kelso, after his team had taken their cuts, sent them onto the field and started slamming grounders at his basemen. He drove one at Olma and watched Johnny Gramner hop to second, take the shortstop's throw, pivot, and fire to Long Sam Aber on first. He belted one to Kevlow and watched the ball go around the horn. Kevlow to Gramner to Aber. And now he realized how slow Arkie Braun had been on second and why Carlton was deep in fourth place with only three weeks of the season played. He smashed a hot grounder to Long Sam, who threw to Johnny Gramner, who threw back to Aber for one of the prettiest double plays in baseball.

The hole, Kelso thought, was plugged up.

Johnny Gramner was feeling good. This was as easy as sitting in a hammock. He wouldn't be in Class C long, he promised himself. Al Sava had told him that contracts did not necessarily tie a man up. If they needed you

22

enough, they'd stand some pressure. At Mrs. Grady's he'd heard that Latham's club was close to bankruptcy, that Latham had poured the profits of his real estate and insurance business into the ball club that was his obsession. For over a year there had seldom been a thousand fans at one game in Farrington Park. What had Al Sava told him? Get them where it hurts and you name your own price.

He remembered West Lancey Street and the tough district around it and vowed he'd never return except to see his mother or to say hello to Al. Most of the small fry there would never get away. They'd join the gangs and be content with their lot until the cops caught up with them. Their tough luck.

An hour later the team had showered. Kelso singled out the dusky pitcher, Mose Watson, a tall, loose-jointed man with a quick grin and a slow drawl. "How do you feel, Mose?"

"Ready." Mose slapped at a fly that buzzed around his head. Kelso went to Mike Saviola, the second-string catcher, and asked him if Mose had looked ready.

"His screwball was working, Dan," the catcher said. "I'd risk starting him."

Johnny Gramner, stripped to the waist, said, "Don't they ever wet down the infield?"

"We've had a drought out here," Joey Olma said. "This isn't Yankee Stadium, kid. We have to fill in our own gopher holes. Wait until you see the tail-enders' ball park."

Dan Kelso watched Johnny closely. There was little respect in the youngster's eyes as he glanced at old-timers like Irv Kevlow, Cy Sheckard, and Mike Saviola. There was a trace of contempt in his analysis, and Kelso

23

had a strong feeling that Latham would pay through the nose for second place in the standings. Thousands of kids in the country, he knew, would have played for board and room alone to have the chance afforded Johnny Gramner, but he knew that if he told this to the boy from Bridge City, it would make no impression. Mechanically he was perfect, it appeared up to now, in his position, but that would not be enough. The heart had to be in this game as well as the mind.

By seven-thirty the fans began trickling into the stands. The visiting league-leaders, the Laraine Robins, were going through fielding practice. They had two pitchers warming up, one of whom, Gus Minot, was the property of the Chicago Bruins. Two days ago he had shut out the Logansville Blues with two hits.

The Carlton Braves filled their dugout. When Kelso sent Mose Watson out to warm up, the fans cheered and booed in about equal proportions. Ox Janosky said, "Bet there's over a thousand in the stands. A curiosity sale."

Johnny clamped his jaws tight and kneaded the glove he had used for the past two years. The brown glove was nearly black now from countless treatments of olive oil. All the padding had been worked out of the palm. He watched Gus Minot throw to his catcher and realized he had never faced that fast a ball. The players around him were already planning their attack on the star right-hander. Ox Janosky said, "He telegraphs his curve. He only pumps once."

"Don't bite at his hook," Long Sam said. "He seldom gets a corner with it. About his fast one, well, just shut your eyes and swing."

24

The Robins cleared the field and the Braves went out and fired the ball around. The fans gave out with an approving hum of sounds as they watched the new Carlton second baseman make the plays at the keystone sack. Just outside third base, Mose Watson, undisturbed by the sound of Minot's fast one cracking into a catcher's mitt, threw easily. One thing Kelso knew—Mose would have control.

At eight o'clock the two banks of lights were turned on. Their yellowish glow barely reached the outfield. A couple of groundkeepers were dragging the infield, and Kelso went to the plate to discuss ground rules with the manager of the Laraine club and the two umpires. He handed his batting order in. The crowd roared impatiently and already some of the fans were calling derisively for Johnny Gramner. They'd loved Arkie Braun, even while he'd booted easy ones and had struck out with the bases loaded.

Kelso thought, These things Johnny will have to learn.

The Braves trotted to their positions. Mose Watson walked slowly out to the pitching hill. Johnny began to feel the pressure. The palms of his hands were moist. None of the other players looked his way. He felt every pair of eyes in the ball park boring through him as he stooped over and picked up a pebble and threw it away. A fan shouted, "He acts like a ballplayer!"

Laughter rippled through the stands, and Johnny glanced toward Long Sam Aber, just off the first sack. Aber was grinning.

A roar went up when Hellman, the Robins' lead-off man, took his stance at the plate. Mose Watson looked him over, studied Janosky's sign, and pumped twice. He fired one straight down the middle, and the fans sat back when it was called a strike. Mose threw one inside that Hellman caught on the bat handle and dribbled to third. Kevlow charged the ball, picked it up, and fired it past Long Sam, and Hellman reached second on the error. Johnny kicked the dirt up, and Mose glared at him.

On the bench, Kelso felt a slow anger.

The dusky hurler got behind the next hitter, then worked the count to three and two. When he got the third strike with a screwball, the fans came to life. Isbell, the Robins' hard-hitting first baseman, took a strike, fouled one off, and let two bad ones go by. The fifth pitch looked good and he swung from his heels. It was a high pop-up just outside the diamond at second base. It was either Olma's or Gramner's ball, and both went after it. The kid from Bridge City paid no attention to Olma's call until it was a moment too late. The shortstop had to make a wild stab at the ball after he had given up on it, and dropped it. Johnny stood frozen to the grass a few feet away while the runner barreled into second base.

The crowd poured it on Johnny. Olma said, "I called for that ball, Gramner."

"Let me take them hereafter," Johnny snapped, and walked away. He took his position and tried not to hear the abuse from the fans, telling himself Olma had been wrong on the play.

Watson was in a hole. Kelso had Fireman McBride throwing in the bull pen. The Laraine cleanup man was waving his black bat at Mose. He'd hit six home runs in ten days.

Johnny looked at Kelso and saw the manager motion toward first base. The shift against Babe Kahlmer sometimes worked. Mose threw the slugger an inside pitch, and the big man jumped back. Mose fired on the outside, and Babe hit it foul in the left-field stands. The stands suffered with every pitch Old Mose made.

Kahlmer cut at the third pitch and drove it high and deep to right field, where Cy Sheckard had taken off with the crack of the bat. Johnny watched the veteran leap high into the air near the foul line and come down with the ball. The runner scored easily from third. But there were two out. Mose forced the next batter to hit his pitch, and the ball scorched to the right of Johnny, who backhanded it, whirled, and threw to Long Sam. There was a smattering of applause in the stands.

"Nice pitching, Mose," Kelso said. "They shouldn't have had a run."

"Whose ball was that?" Johnny suddenly asked, his chin thrust out.

Kelso said, as Joey Olma went out to lead off for the Braves, "Wait him out, kid."

"Let's hope he's wild," Ox Janosky said.

"And get killed?" Hank Rawson, the center fielder said. "I would rather live and strike out."

Johnny set his mouth hard and looked into the artificial light.

Olma struck out on four pitched balls. He threw his bat halfway to the dugout, said to Cy Sheckard, "I cut at one a mile outside. Watch 'em." Johnny knelt in the slot as the right fielder dug in against Gus Minot, and insisted to himself that he'd had a right to that fly ball off second.

Sheckard worked the string out on Minot. He refused to swing at a low curve and walked to first. Kelso, coaching at third, clapped his hands. "Let's go, Johnny!"

27

The fans went to work on him. He stood at the plate and watched the Laraine right-hander turn his back and rub up the ball. The Robins on the bench began to needle. They were experienced bench jockeys, and one of them had often riled a man named Leo Durocher.

"What's his name, Pete, Grammy?"

"He stands like Grandma Moses, don't he?"

"Toss it underhand, Gus. I have a soft heart."

Johnny waited, trying to shake off the barbs. They were biting him deep when Minot threw one down the middle. The ball was a blur and he struck at it and missed.

"The insects are thick around here tonight," a Laraine joker shouted from the dugout.

He dug in again, watching Minot carefully. The fastballer threw one on the inside corner, and the umpire called it a strike. Johnny whirled away from the plate, his eyes fiery. The Robin catcher said, "Easy, kid. You're new around here."

The fans joined the bench jockeys. Dan Kelso called Johnny away from the plate and talked to him. "You're digging your own grave, Gramner. Keep your head!"

Johnny went back to the plate and struck out; he came back to the bench to the tune of the crowd's mocking chant. "Call Arkie back!" a fan off first yelled.

"Don't act as if you had committed a murder," Mose Watson said. "Everybody strikes out."

Hank Rawson, batting in the cleanup spot tonight, managed to belt Minot's second pitch deep to center, where the Robin fielder gathered it in after a hard run.

"So he *can* be hit," Kelso said as he came back to the bench.

The game developed into a pitchers' duel. At the end

of seven innings there was that one Laraine run. The Robins had pecked away at Old Mose for five singles, and the Braves owned but a scratch hit and a double.

The Laraine shortstop led off in the eighth and crowded the plate on Mose. Anything to get on at this stage of the game. The Carlton hurler worked too carefully on the man and lost him. Immediately Long Sam and Irv Kevlow moved in for the expected bunt. The batter dragged one along the first-base line, and Aber raced in and scooped it up. His only throw was to first base, where Johnny Gramner covered. The Robins had a base runner at the pickup spot.

Kelso, after Mose had a ball and a strike on the next batter, gave the sign for the waste pitch. The base runner had a big lead off the bag. Mose fired wide. Janosky took it and fired down to the keystone sack, but the ball went out into center field, and the crowd groaned its dismay as the runner went to third. Rawson had charged in from shallow center, and the Laraine coach held his man up, gambling on a long fly for the important run.

Olma walked toward the bag as Mose stepped off the rubber. "You didn't see the sign, Gramner?"

"I can't get them overnight," Johnny fired back.

A Robin long-ball hitter lofted Mose Watson's third pitch to deep right. Sheckard fired in to the plate, but the second run of the game came over. Kelso sat back in the dugout staring out at Johnny Gramner, a small smile on his face. It was worth losing a game, he thought, to prove to a young player how little he knew about baseball. Gramner had not stopped learning the hard way.

Mose took a come-backer from the bat of the Robins'

29

left fielder and threw him out. He walked into the bench, unperturbed, and Johnny Gramner wondered why. Winning games is a pitcher's bread and butter. Dan Kelso could have told him why. Mose was a human being, a great gentleman who judged that any man was entitled to a few mistakes.

The Braves bench was quiet as Long Sam Aber threw the loaded bat away and walked up to face Gus Minot with his big yellow bat. Long Sam had been in a slump and the crowd was yelling encouragement. Old Mose said, "That's a new bat. There's a hit in it, Long Sam!"

Aber drove Minot's first pitch through the box and over second for a single, and Flit Buhel stepped in. Flit was hitting .224. Dan Kelso called him back and motioned Leo Masi, his utility man, off the bench. "Drag one," he said under his breath.

Masi fouled two tries off, then bunted too vigorously; Minot raced off the mound and caught it before it hit the grass. Long Sam was halfway to second and fell as he tried to get back. Minot doubled him off.

Irv Kevlow struck out. He passed the Robin pitcher on his way out to his position and said something to him. Minot said something back and grinned. Dan Kelso wished that Gramner would watch those little angles. They'd do wonders putting him on the right road.

In the top of the ninth Kahlmer hit one far over the fence in right, and Kelso guessed that insurance run was all Minot would need. Well, they wouldn't have to look at him again for a while. Mose got the next three batters out, Gramner making a leaping catch of a bullet drive that was labeled two bases.

"Nice catch, Johnny," Mose said, walking in with the fielder.

30

The second sacker chewed fast on his gum, stared straight ahead, trying to remember a ball game where he hadn't made a semblance of a hit. "So what?" he said to the pitcher. "They pay off in this business with base hits."

Mose eyed Johnny askance, said no more.

Minot had no trouble with the Braves in the last of the ninth. He walked off the field with a three-hitter, and the fans were silent on their way from the wooden stands. Johnny Gramner left the dugout behind Mose and Dan Kelso. "You pitched a strong game, Mose," the manager said. "We'll try to even things up with Hooks Grozek in there tomorrow."

In the locker room, Matt Yager came up to Johnny. "I had my story all written, kid. You let me down. Where was that home run?"

"Leave me alone!" Johnny Gramner said angrily. "Go peddle your papers!"

"Yeah," the writer said. "It'll be a pleasure."

The other players glanced toward the new infielder without comment. Dan Kelso, on his way to the shower, realized that a man could also make errors off the field, miscues that were more damaging than those that let in runs. Such errors probably kept more men out of the majors than those appearing in the box scores. And a manager often had no way of correcting them.

CHAPTER 3

At eleven o'clock the next morning Kelso called at Mrs. Grady's and knocked on the rookie's door. Johnny Gramner's mood indicated a lack of sleep, a childish irritation. "All right, Kelso, answer me now. Who should have caught that pop fly?"

"Olma," Dan said. "He called you off. You should have run back to the bag to cover so that the base runner would have to stay on first in case the ball was dropped, which it was. It's elementary baseball, Johnny. Even the Little Leaguers know that."

"I never bothered with that toy game," Johnny shot back.

"You missed more than you know," Kelso said. "And hereafter watch my signals, Gramner. Kicking up the dirt when a player makes an error isn't done where men play ball. You're green. You were expected to be, but the team will give you every chance to come through."

"I'll look after myself, Kelso. Tell those guys!"

"We'll see, Johnny. You came out of Bridge City with a chip on your shoulder, and you'll blame everything on circumstances and environment when things go wrong. Only a man who lacks character uses that excuse. If you only knew the chance you've got to—"

"I don't like preaching, Kelso," Johnny cut in. "If I flop I won't ask you for another chance."

32

"Maybe Al Sava?" the manager said.

"Maybe." Johnny fired a shoe against the wall. Then he whirled around. "What do you know about Sava?"

"Nothing yet," Dan Kelso said. "But if I had a kid brother, I'd worry about his working for that guy."

"Rick can take care of himself," Johnny said. "The way I did. The way I always will."

Dan gave him a long look. "O.K.," he said finally, "and good luck tonight." Going down the stairs, he reminded himself he was working on a fresh ballplayer and not a case history. His salary did not call for welfare work.

It was a perfect night for baseball, but Kelso was sure there were not more than a thousand people in Farrington Park. The Carlton fans had known prolonged pennant famine and their patience was near exhaustion. They had watched Johnny Gramner and had been unimpressed. In his little office under the stands, Kelso shifted his line-up on paper and studied it:

> Olma, ss
> Masi, 3b
> Sheckhard, rf
> Rawson, cf
> Aber, 1b
> Janosky, c
> Gramner, 2b
> Buhel, lf

He'd rest Irv Kevlow. The man was forty if he was a day—a real octogenarian in baseball. Ben Farrel of the Robins would undoubtedly work his southpaw, Vic O'Day, tonight.

He went into the musty locker room and immediately felt the absence of old Arkie Braun. Arkie was always ready with a joke, a word or two that could lift a slumping player out of the deep rut. Kelso announced his line-up, and Kevlow grinned dryly. "I'll check the rubber tips of my crutches during the rest, Dan."

Johnny Gramner sat on the bench in front of the battered lockers, pounding a fist into the palm of his glove and envying the Laraine Robins. They were six games in front and could easily pull away out of sight. Why hadn't Farrel come to comb the sand lots of Bridge City?

"All right," Kelso said. "Hooks, go on out and warm up."

A few minutes later the other players went out to the runway. Just as they reached the dugout, Kelso stepped up behind Johnny and put a hand on the kid's shoulder. "It's going to be O.K., Johnny. When you get that first hit, you'll see."

"Yeah," the second baseman said, and went to the water cooler.

When the Carlton team took the field the greeting from the stands was a little sour. A lot of the customers got on Kelso's new infielder and rode him hard.

Hooks Grozek started strong and struck out the first two Robin hitters. The third man smashed his change-up to the left of Johnny Gramner, and the rookie raced into the hole, came up with the ball, and threw to Long Sam Aber for a close put-out. There was scattered applause. A fan yelled, "Good field, no hit!"

Johnny took his place on the bench, sure he wouldn't take a cut in the first inning. When Olma

34

picked up his bat, Kelso said, "Start us off, Joey." He went out to the coach's box.

O'Day was wild. He couldn't find the plate and Olma walked. Leo Masi worked the southpaw to a full count and then hit O'Day's fast one to right field for a long single, and Olma galloped all the way to third. The crowd came alive and called for a big inning. Sheckard crowded the plate, and after O'Day brushed his letters with his fourth pitch, trotted to first. The bags were loaded and Hank Rawson was at the plate. The Laraine manager sent a right-hander out to warm up.

Johnny Gramner hoped Hank would get on and give him a chance to get up there. The cleanup hitter swung at O'Day's first pitch and drove it through a wide-open space in the Laraine outfield. It rolled to the fence and three runs came across. The old stands of Farrington Park seemed to sway as the fans cut loose. Kelso, off third, clapped his hands and yelled, "Keep us goin', Sam!"

Long Sam took a strike, ducked one right at his head, and powdered the next delivery deep to center, where the Robin infielder gathered it in. Rawson trotted back to second. Johnny Gramner, his determined chin as hard as a rock, followed Ox Janosky. He knelt in the slot and watched the big catcher take three wide ones, miss a low, sweeping curve, and then drop into the dust when O'Day fired close to his head. Ox got up, said something to the Robin pitcher as he trotted to first.

The crowd booed when Johnny faced the Robin left-hander. O'Day's batterymate called time and went to the mound to talk to his pitcher. The rookie from Bridge City rubbed some dirt against the palms of his cold

35

moist hands. The Laraine bench laced into him. Kelso called down from third, "Get a good one, Johnny!" The Braves bench was silent.

Johnny watched a curve come at him and kept his bat on his shoulder. It missed the corner, but O'Day jumped off the hill to protest the umpire's call. He finally cooled off and fired one low and into the dirt that the catcher managed to knock down. Johnny looked at Kelso and got the take sign. O'Day's pitch was right down the middle; Johnny Gramner swung and drove it high and deep to left center. The Laraine fielders suddenly stopped running. The ball was over the fence for a home run.

The stands were in an uproar as the rookie rounded third. Kelso stood immobile in the coach's box and watched Long Sam and Ox go into the dugout after they had scored ahead of the blast, ignoring the time-honored greeting at home plate. The players in the dugout did not get up when Johnny ducked under the low-hanging roof. Hank Rawson said, "That'll cost you ten, rookie!"

"Worth it," Johnny said. "It was my pitch. Hits are what keep a ballplayer alive."

The Laraine pilot was at the mound with his catcher and three infielders. He called in the right-hander, and O'Day walked off, getting his lumps from the home fans.

Johnny looked at Kelso and grinned. Let him fine me, he thought. I'll get it back a hundredfold.

Enzman, the right-hander, got Buhel and Hooks Grozek to ground out, and the Braves took the field with a six-run lead over the league-leaders.

Grozek breezed along for five innings, limiting the Robins to three hits. In the top of the sixth he began to tire and walked the first two men. When Kahlmer, the

36

league's home-run hitter, stepped in, the fans began to squirm and yell for a new pitcher.

Joey Olma, Masi, and Long Sam talked it up. Johnny Gramner shifted toward first and deep, going along with Kelso's shift against the power hitter.

Kahlmer wasted no time. He belted Grozek's first pitch to deep right, and Sheckard started running. Dan Kelso came out to the top step of the dugout and yelled at Johnny. The rookie was glued to the edge of the grass, watching. Sheckard tried for an over-the-shoulder catch, but the ball eluded him and rolled to the fence. It was Joey Olma who ran out for the relay and managed to fire to Masi at third to prevent Kahlmer from getting an inside-the-park home run. The shortstop looked at Johnny and shook his head.

Grozek settled down, got the next man to pop to shallow right, and Kahlmer held up at third. Hooks lived up to his name when he got the next batter on strikes, and the crowd settled back and let out a massed sigh of relief. The Robin left fielder skied to Rawson, and that was all for the Laraine offense.

Kelso turned to Irv Kevlow. "Coach at third for the rest of the way," he said. He waited until Johnny Gramner came in and sat down. "Why weren't you out there for a relay when you saw that ball might not have been caught? Didn't they teach you that when a long ball is hit to right, the second baseman goes out on the grass?"

"I'll remember that," Johnny said, and also remembered the cheers from the crowd when he'd hit the home run. He stared straight ahead, chewing on his gum, ignoring Kelso. The bat paid off, mister. Remember the

Babe. Ask Ted Williams. The Splinter never got paid for his fielding.

The Braves had their hitting suits on. Dawson opened the Braves' half with a double along the left-field foul line. Long Sam singled off the Robin shortstop's glove, and Hank came in to score in a cloud of dust. Johnny Gramner picked up a bat when Janosky stepped to the plate. Ox slammed Enzman's second pitch to third, where the Robin fielder dug it out neatly and fired around the horn for a fast double play.

The fans cut loose when the rookie took his stance at the plate. Enzman fed him a wide one and slipped over a change-of-pace ball. Confident now, Johnny stepped into Enzman's curve and got it solid on the meat end of his bat. It sailed on a line to left and rattled off the fence, and Johnny went all the way to third standing up. He stood grinning at Leo Masi in the coach's box. "Maybe that will cost me five," he said.

"Your hat is still too small, Gramner," Masi said.

Buhel, a weak hitter, got the fever and bounced a single through the box. Johnny Gramner scored Carlton's eighth run while the fans tore up the pea patch. The Braves made room for him on the bench, displaying no more emotion than if he'd just struck out. They resent the competition, Johnny thought, and laughed inside. He picked up his glove when Hooks struck out, and ran out to second base.

Kahlmer got his home run in the eighth with the bases empty, and Carlton, having their best night for a long time, came back with three more runs of their own, one driven in by Johnny Gramner. The rookie threw a derisive gesture toward the Laraine dugout when he reached first base, and the crowd roared with delight.

Dan Kelso looked up at the scoreboard that showed Carlton leading, 11–3, and wished he could be as happy about it as the fans.

In the top of the ninth, Hooks took care of the Robins and the Braves trotted off the field with a big win. In the dugout, Kelso took Johnny by the arm as the rookie was turning toward the runway. "Wait, I want to talk to you."

"Look," Johnny said, with the fans still buzzing overhead. "I'll pay you the fine. I could have taken that pitch and never got another as fat. Buhel was coming up, a weak hitter. He could have—"

"I manage this team, Gramner!" Dan Kelso felt his temper getting away from him. "Don't ever forget it. And if you ever refuse to take another sign from me I'll—"

"Bench me? I got three hits tonight, Mr. Kelso," Johnny said. "That's what the crowd comes out to see. They will tear you apart if you take me out of that line-up. All right, we'll both come out on top. You'll get a raise if we win the pennant. I get a bonus if I hit over three hundred. We're both in business."

Kelso said, "I see. You have another manager, Johnny. He knows all the angles."

"I guess he learned them the hard way, too, Mr. Kelso. You got something to sell, they'll buy it." He shoved his glove into his pocket and went out to the runway.

Kelso followed him. "And the kids outside the gate looking for autographs, Johnny. That's a business?"

"Sure," the ballplayer said. "I got one once from Minnie Minoso. I sold it to a kid for a jackknife and a stack of comic books."

"Gramner," Dan Kelso said, "I feel sorry for you."

Later, outside Farrington Park, Kelso sat in his car, watching the rookie who had been mobbed by the kids just outside the players' entrance. They were thrusting everything his way that could be written on, and he was standing there without an outward sign of impatience. Kelso wished the lights had been stronger so he could have had a clearer look at Johnny's face. As he turned on the ignition he smiled a little and remembered a scandal that had taken place when he had been only a kid himself. One of those players had told the reporters afterward that the thing that made him repent the most was the look in the eyes of the kids who had gathered outside the criminal courts building. Driving home, the Carlton manager decided to withhold judgment and hold back Johnny Gramner's fine.

CHAPTER 4

THE CARLTON BRAVES TOOK THE RUBBER GAME FROM the league-leaders, 10–9, in a free-hitting affair. The next morning the team was on the bus heading for Wooster, home of the fifth-place Buckeyes. Johnny read the Carlton *Advertiser* as the bus roared west. He tore out the box score that showed he had made three more hits against the Robins, one a triple, and had knocked in three runs. He'd hit .461 for the first series with Carlton.

40

"Starting a scrapbook?" Joey Olma, sitting beside him, asked.

"I'm sending this to a friend," Johnny said. "I'll bet you five I don't get fined this week."

"I never make bets," the shortstop said. "How do the standings look?"

"Take a look." Johnny handed him the sports page.

"They say nice things about you," Olma said. "It's always O.K. when you get your hits."

"My friend always told me that."

Joey studied the standing of the clubs:

	W.	L.	Pct.
Laraine	16	9	.640
Freeport	13	12	.520
Logansville	11	14	.440
CARLTON	10	14	.416
Wooster	10	15	.400
Portsmouth	7	17	.292

"We're five and a half games behind," the shortstop said. "That's a lot to make up."

"We'll be in second place after this trip." Johnny leaned back in his seat and wondered how it felt to fly in the big planes. A lot of the big league teams took to the air. They also ate steaks and slept at the best hotels. The television cameras were on them when they went up to hit or made a fielding play, and guys like Yogi Berra got plenty of money from endorsements. It was a business all right.The buses and the tacky hotels were not too bad for a beginning, but how could men like Kevlow and Janosky come back to it after the lush days?

Nearly two thousand people turned out at the Wooster

41

ball park that night to see Johnny Gramner hit a home run and a double. Hank Rawson and Ox Janosky also connected with the circuit, and Mose Watson gave up only five scattered hits to win, 10–1.

In the lobby of the Commercial House that night, Johnny felt very good. The transients stared at him. He heard a salesman say, "That's the Braves' new second baseman. Quite a hitter." Joey Olma and Flit Buhel came out of the old cable elevator and invited him to go to the movies.

"And see Pola Negri or Fatty Arbuckle?" Johnny snorted. "Where can we get a fast game of pool?"

"It's a joint," Buhel said. "Near the tracks. Keep away from it, Gramner."

"Or you'll tell Kelso?" Johnny grinned and walked out of the hotel. He found the pool parlor and had his game. A town character, a Buckeye fan, paid the second baseman his losses and said, "Maybe you'll gimme a chance to get my dough back, Gramner. I'll lay you two to one you don't get but one hit off Speed Seskin tomorrow night."

"I'll take it," Johnny said.

The incident was reported in the paper the next afternoon in a particularly caustic sports column. There was method in the writer's madness—it would put pressure on the Braves' rookie and thereby help Wooster's cause. Dan Kelso stormed into Johnny's room two hours before game time. He found the second sacker sprawled on the bed, reading the paper.

"Are you out of your mind, Gramner?" Kelso snapped.

"It's good publicity." Johnny shrugged. "If you're talking about that sports column."

"You won't win or lose," the manager yelled. "You

42

sit on the bench tonight. You know the rules on this club about betting. They apply to every man on this ball club."

Johnny sat up, his eyes wide. He threw the paper to the floor. "You're kidding, Kelso."

"Guess again, Johnny. This time it will cost you ten dollars."

"I'll see Latham," the player said, his temper rising. "I'll tell him to make a deal with some other club."

"Go right ahead." Kelso turned on his heel and walked out.

The Braves suited up at seven thirty. When Kelso told Leo Masi he would be at second base, the other Carlton players stopped what they were doing and stared at him. Ox Janosky slammed his glove to the bench, and his mates knew what he was thinking. The league-leaders were playing the tough Logansville Blues and here was a chance to climb. Masi had never hit over two sixty in his life.

Hank Rawson said, "The people out there won't like this, Dan."

"Too bad, Hank," Kelso said. "They don't manage this club."

Speed Seskin put the Braves down in order in the first half of the inning, and then a ripple of displeasure ran through the stands when they realized that the Carlton rookie was not playing. Johnny, sitting beside Mose Watson, grinned. He felt even better when the Buckeyes teed off against Tony Rocca, starting in the box for Carlton. Three runs were in, there were men on first and third and only one out when Kelso left the dugout. He called in Fireman McBride. The first batter to face

43

the new pitcher skied to right and another run scored. McBride got the next man to roll to Long Sam Aber at first base.

Seskin's curve was hitting the corners, and his side-arm delivery was handcuffing Kelso's hitters. At the end of the sixth, Wooster was leading, 5–0. The fans yelled for Johnny Gramner every time Leo Masi came up. In the fifth Masi had booted a possible double-play ball and had handed the Buckeyes an unearned run.

Hank Rawson led off for the Braves in the top of the seventh and immediately hit the first pitch and drove it out of the park. The blow unsettled Seskin and he walked Long Sam after the big first basemen had fouled off five pitches. Ox Janosky hit a blooper over the Buckeye infield and two were on.

The stands buzzed, expecting to see the Carlton rookie hit for Masi. When Leo came out, the crowd banged their feet against the planks and booed.

Johnny leaned forward to watch Masi take two called strikes, and he glanced at Dan Kelso, coaching off third. The manager clapped his hands. "Get a good ball, Leo," he called out.

Speed Seskin pumped twice, threw his fast ball, and Masi swung hard. The ball scorched past the Buckeye third baseman close to the line, and Long Sam and Janosky scored before the ball was relayed in from deep left. Johnny set his lips hard and watched Kelso. Now the pitcher was coming up with a chance to get the game even. The fans were buzzing again. Kelso let McBride hit, and a roar went up. Mose said, "He sure sticks by his guns, Dan does."

McBride struck out, and Joey Olma came up and popped to the catcher.

When Kelso came in, Johnny said to Mose, "It was given away."

The manager said, "We have two more tries, Gramner."

McBride, after getting into a hole, was saved by a double play in the last half of the inning. Irv Kevlow, playing third for the Braves, led off the eighth, and drew a pass. Sheckard grounded to first, a lazy hopper that enabled Kevlow to reach second, and Hank Rawson stepped in. The catcher went out to the mound, looked toward the Buckeye bench. They got the signal to pass the Carlton long-ball hitter with first base open. They could gamble for the twin killing.

But Long Sam Aber crossed up the Wooster strategy with a clean single to right field, and Kevlow came in with the Braves' fourth run. Hank Rawson raced to third. Again the Buckeye battery conferred; Speed Seskin was ordered to walk Ox Janosky and pitch to the deep bottom of the Carlton batting order.

Johnny Gramner looked for a sign from Kelso, but it didn't come. Leo Masi went up to hit. The second sacker took a strike, fouled one past third, then was called out looking at the next pitch.

Flit Buhel glanced at Kelso after running the count to three balls and one strike. He got the take sign and let Seskin's pitch go by. A strike. Buhel was on his own now, and Johnny Gramner wondered what Matt Yager would say about Kelso in the Carlton *Advertiser* tomorrow for throwing this one away.

Crack! Buhel drove one over short and two runs came in, putting Carlton out in front, 6–5.

"How lucky can you get?" Johnny growled.

45

Mose Watson eyed him without humor. "What was that, friend?" he said.

McBride hit to the pitcher and was thrown out. The fireman, with a one-run lead, went out and got the Buckeyes in order. Dan Kelso walked over to the third-base coaching box, and Johnny Gramner felt like leaving the dugout, peeling off his suit, and heading back to Bridge City. "I don't get it," he muttered.

"Some day maybe you will, Johnny," Mose Watson said. "You got to play it right off the field, too."

Joey Olma drew a walk, but Kevlow and Sheckard flied out. Hank Rawson stepped in and swung hard at Speed Seskin's first two pitches. McBride said, "Belt one, Hank. I need more than a run."

The slugger must have heard the fireman. He hit Seskin's next pitch to the center-field fence for a double, and Olma ran all the way home. Long Sam lined out to third.

The last half of the ninth was rough. With two gone, McBride walked the Wooster center fielder, and Long Sam Aber bobbled a hard shot just off the bag. The Buckeye's cleanup hitter singled sharply past Leo Masi, and the score was now 7–6 in the Braves' favor. Dan Kelso called in Hooks Grozek to relieve. The crowd yelled for another hit when Hooks took the ball from McBride.

Hooks threw two bad ones and in the bull pen Whitey DeLong kept warming up. Hooks got his curve over, then whipped his fast one by. Kelso yelled out, "One more, Hooks, and we go home!" The pitcher looked in and grinned. He fired the fast one again, high and wide, but the overanxious Buckeye hitter took a good cut and missed.

46

Leo Masi limped into the locker room. An old Charley horse had come back to plague him. Kelso said, "You'll get a rest. Johnny Gramner will take over again tomorrow."

The rookie jerked his head around. "You sure, Mr. Kelso?"

The manager looked Johnny straight in the eye. "Very sure," he said.

When they got to the hotel, they learned that the Blues had beaten the league-leaders, and Mose Watson said, "Maybe after ten years I'll know how it feels to be in the first division, Dan."

"They'll be tough. The Robins will bring in talent from their mother club if they need it," Kelso said. "We have to go along with what we've got."

Johnny Gramner went into the elevator; he looked forward to reading tomorrow's paper. He was pretty certain he'd enjoy reading it.

An hour after lunch, the second baseman picked up the paper and sat in the lobby to read the sports page. At first he wondered if he'd read the type correctly. It said in part: ". . . *Kelso's benching of his rookie sensation, Johnny Gramner, took more than a little courage on his part, and this writer, aware of the reason for his disciplinary action, highly commends him. This game of baseball is bigger than the individual. It is a dignified profession with its own moral code, whether it be played in New York or Wooster. The conduct of one player can easily. . . .*"

Johnny threw the paper aside and went out into the street. Mose Watson strolled away from the desk to pick it up. Hank Rawson joined him a few moments later.

"An' so endeth the first lesson," Mose said. "He's a good boy, Hank. Jus' needs a little straightenin' around is all. He got a chip on his shoulder an' when it's knocked off you won't see no more sign of wood higher up no more."

"I know that neighborhood in Bridge City, Mose," Hank said. "You don't start off even with the world there. No silver spoon in your mouth when you're born. Most likely you feel the end of a night stick in your ribs."

On Sunday afternoon the Wooster fans got a good look at Johnny Gramner. At the end of the fifth they were wishing that Kelso had benched him for keeps. He had cut off a promising Buckeye rally in the third with a circus catch behind the keystone sack and had knocked in two runs with a homer over the right-field wire screen. In the last of the fifth he had taken a hot shot far to his left, tagged a runner coming from first, and thrown to Long Sam for the double play.

"Good going, Johnny," Kelso said when the Braves came to bat in the first of the sixth.

The fielder said nothing. He was thinking of the ten dollar bill the Carlton club had held out of his pay, and a letter he had received from Al Sava yesterday morning. *They'll push you around if you're sucker enough to let 'em. A ball club owns you body and soul, kid. They'll swap you like you were a horse or a cow if you don't keep delivering. . . .*

He watched Flit Buhel ground weakly to short and squirmed on the bench when Whitey DeLong, the pitcher, struck out swinging. Joey Olma waved at a curve, then skied to center. Why did they stay in the game, Johnny wondered. They were going nowhere. A guy could make a hundred or more bucks every week driving

48

a truck or working a lathe and wouldn't have to ride buses or eat the garbage they gave you in whistle-stop hotels and cheap restaurants. Somebody should tell them.

Johnny Gramner led off in the eighth, and the rabid home crowd called on their left-hander to strike him out. He caught a curve ball right and sent it screaming past the Buckeye first baseman to the right-field corner. He was rounding second when the relay came in and thudded into the Wooster second baseman's glove and Kelso yelled for him to hold up. He streaked for third, hit the dirt, and caught a flash of the ball beating him in. He kicked it out of the baseman's hands and it rolled to the stands. He got up and raced home and the crowd began to boo.

Dan Kelso walked up and down the coach's box, his eyes blazing, knowing that he could cut off his nose and spite his face if he kept disciplining this rookie from Bridge City. Gramner was the difference this year, he knew. He was a ballplayer, one of those rare ones that come up only once in ten years. He'd have to swallow his pride. Even Stengel and Durocher did not bench a four-hundred hitter, not unless the hitter committed a major crime.

The run proved to be the difference. The Wooster Buckeyes knocked DeLong out in the ninth, and Mose had to go out and cool them off. There were two on, only one out, and two runs in when he struck out the Buckeye catcher. Johnny Gramner backhanded a hot smash close to the bag and forced the man coming down from first for the ball game. As he ran off he wondered if Kelso would be sore about his not holding up at second on that last hit. And then he saw the Wooster third baseman coming toward him, fire in his eye. He was a big man, nearly six feet tall.

"You fresh rookie!" the fielder said, and the umpires and a policeman came running.

Johnny Gramner stopped. "What's the beef?" he asked, knowing full well what it was. He glanced around him, saw none of the Carlton players moving in. He threw up his hands when the Buckeye player sailed in at him, and a fist caught him in the shoulder and spun him half around. Half of the Wooster team pulled the third baseman away, and the cop said, "Get goin', Gramner!"

He came into the dugout and looked at the Carlton players. "You hoped that big lug would murder me!" he said, and rubbed his left shoulder.

Mose Watson said, "We never figured you needed help, Johnny."

Kelso said, "Let me look at the shoulder, Johnny." He went to a locker and took out a bottle of liniment. "You played a little rough. They dished it back to you."

"O.K.," Johnny said. "I'll keep looking out for myself." He sat on the table and let Kelso rub the bruise on his shoulder. It felt as if a wooden mallet had struck it, and suddenly he felt his blood grow cold. The shoulder could easily have been broken. The players dressed and left in small groups. "Why do they dislike me?" the rookie suddenly asked.

"They don't," the manager said. "It's all in your mind, Johnny. You take out only what you put into anything in this life. Most of them have lived twice as long as you. Anything you want to know bad enough, anything, they can all tell you. One or the other."

"What would *I* ask them?" Johnny said.

"Right now? I wouldn't know. Later, there could be many things," Dan Kelso said.

Johnny shook his head. It made no sense to him.

The Carlton ball club went to Logansville for a Monday night game, and before two innings had been played, it was apparent that the opposition was trying to cool off Johnny Gramner. A base runner came in at him and spilled him hard after he'd taken a toss from Joey Olma, and he had been unable to get the ball to Long Sam for the twin killing. He got up and walked around, and Tony Rocca, pitching for the Braves, went out and looked him over. "Go back and pitch," Johnny told him. "I'm all right." And he glared at the Logansville player who had knocked him down.

In the sixth, with the Blues in front, 2–0, he cut back in behind a Blue base runner, took a bullet throw from Ox Janosky, and was dumped again, while tagging the man out. This time he felt the sting of a spike wound, and knelt on one knee for a while looking at the blood on the back of his hand.

"Sorry," the Logansville base runner said before he went back to his bench. "Knocking you over was intentional. Spiking you, no!"

Dan Kelso sat on the bench, taking the hard lumps with Johnny, praying that he wouldn't be injured. The fans were enjoying the proceedings and yelling for more. A few moments later the flash from Bridge City went high into the air and pulled a screaming liner down and doubled a man off third.

In the seventh inning Johnny Gramner came up to hit, batting in third position in place of Sheckard, who had been dropped down to sixth in the batting order. Joey

Olma was on second and one man was out. Carlton needed two runs to tie. He took two balls, let a good one go by, then looked toward Kelso for the sign. The manager was giving none, and Johnny grinned. The Blues' third baseman was deep. The pitch came in and he suddenly shortened up and sent a trickler down the third-base line. He was crossing first base almost before the Logansville pitcher had picked up the ball that refused to roll foul.

Dan Kelso looked at Johnny and had to grin.

Hank Rawson slammed one at the Logansville short-stop, and the man went for the double play. Johnny, eyes blazing, streaked to second and threw a body block on the Blues' keystone man just as the ball hit his glove. He was out, but he had smeared the double play and a run had scored. The Logansville second baseman got up quickly, and Johnny got ready for battle. And then his mouth dropped open when the player grinned at him. "O.K., kid. That's one for you," he said.

He dusted off his pants and trotted to the bench. "He was yellow," he said to Mose Watson as he sat down.

The pitcher said, "Look, boy, you don't figure this out at all. That boy out there, Lennister, knocked Hank Rawson out cold last year for knockin' him over. You think it over, Johnny."

Ox Janosky took a wide one, went into the dirt from a duster, and then got his first home run in a week over the left-field fence. Carlton went ahead, 3–2.

Hank came into the dugout and looked at Johnny. "You don't know how lucky you are, mister. Lennister won't let you get away with it twice."

Sheckard fanned. The game ended without further scoring, and the Carlton team, enjoying its longest winning streak in over a year, hurried off the field for the cool showers.

Kelso got to the Logansville House a half hour after the others, along with Irv Kevlow, the old veteran. He saw Johnny Gramner with the bulky oily-faced man from Bridge City, Al Sava. Both were on the way to the elevator.

"Come on up for a few minutes, Al," Johnny was saying to the man.

"Yeah, Johnny. You sure made a bum of that Logansville second sacker," Sava replied. "They're all talking about you in Bridge City. You could go back an' be mayor. Say, tell me, you pretty sure the Braves can win the—?"

Kelso said, "The man's no good, Irv. I know it."

"That pigeon-toed walk of his," Kevlow said. "Somewhere I met a man—"

Kelso glanced at the third baseman quickly. "That's odd, Irv. I had the same feeling when I first spotted him. Look, do me a favor. Watch that kid for me until Sava leaves town."

"A pleasure," Kevlow said, his eyes half closed, his mind groping back to the big league parks.

"What do you think of the rookie now, Irv?" Kelso asked as they crossed the lobby together.

"In three years, or maybe less, he'll be in the majors," Kevlow said.

CHAPTER 5

T HE BRAVES CAME HOME ONLY FOUR GAMES OUT OF
first place to play the tail-end Portsmouth club a double-
header on a Saturday afternoon. For the first time in
over two years, Farrington Park was full, and when
Johnny Gramner came out of the dugout for infield
practice, he knew why the crowd was there. He was
hitting .398 and had banged four homers since coming
out of Bridge City. On Monday morning he would pay
George C. Latham a call.

Mose Watson warmed up for the home team. A new
pitcher would start for the Portsmouth Colts, a gangly
high school kid from Massillon.

"Man," Kevlow said to Kelso, "they don't draw a
crowd like this in Philly these days."

"That's right." Kelso wished he could be happier about
it. He watched Johnny Gramner out on the diamond and
knew the kid was making every move a picture. He was
the star attraction and was reveling in it. During the last
few days he had become what baseball players call a
take-charge guy. An important asset to any club if there
is no arrogance involved, but when Dan Kelso heard the
second baseman tell Aber to show more life after missing
a high throw, he felt forebodings.

"Long Sam will step on him like a bug some day,"
Fireman McBride said.

The capacity crowd roared when the rejuvenated
Braves ran out onto the field at one thirty. Johnny tarried

54

for a few moments in the dugout to rinse his mouth with water, and Kelso wondered. He thought he understood when the rookie ran out to his position, all eyes upon him. The cheers lasted until the first Colt batter took his place at the plate. Johnny danced around just off second and a little deep, and yelled, "Come on, Old Mose! Let's take 'em!"

The fans loved it. Kelso caught himself wishing the lead-off man would drive one right through Johnny's legs, and suddenly he was angry at himself. This rookie had been the hypo the Braves had needed, and everybody on the team would benefit, including himself.

Mose fooled the Colt lead-off man with a change of pace after the first two pitches had been fouled off. The dusky hurler worked methodically, taking his time. He straightened his cap, adjusted his trousers, and fooled with the rosin bag. The Portsmouth batter worked Mose to the full count, then banged one hard to the right side. Johnny Gramner raced into the hole, gloved the ball, and fired to Long Sam. The play brought loud applause although it was routine. Mose induced the next hitter to lift one high to right field, where Sheckard took it after moving in a few steps.

Kelso had his batting order about set now. It was the winning combination and he would go along with it. Olma, Sheckard, Gramner, Rawson, Janosky, Aber, Kevlow, Buhel, and the pitcher. The shortstop faced the new Portsmouth pitcher, let the first one go by. Willie "Rube" Furber, the pitcher, cut loose with a fast one that brought gasps from the Braves in the dugout. Olma swung after it was in the Colts' catcher's big mitt.

"Another Feller?" Hank Rawson asked, and looked at Leo Masi.

Joey Olma struck out swinging. Passing Cy Sheckard

on his way from the plate, he grinned ruefully and shook his head. A few minutes later Sheckard walked away after looking at a called third strike. He said to Johnny Gramner, "You can't see it."

Now the two rookies faced each other. There was a big lazy grin on Furber's face. Gramner's chin was thrust out, his eyes deadly serious. He let the blazing fast one go by and the umpire said, "Strike!" He leaned down and got dirt on his hand, then dug in again. The rookie right-hander pumped twice, then cut loose. Gramner tied himself into a knot trying to hit the ball that Furber had put a string on. The Colts' bench began to needle.

Johnny refused to bite at the next two pitches, both of which had been intentionally bad. And then Furber reared back and fired one through that the Braves' second baseman swung at and missed. The fans gave the rookie from Massillon a big hand when he walked off the mound. Kelso came in from the coach's box and grinned dryly at Fireman McBride. "That farmer boy can steal this show," he said.

"It happens," the pitcher said.

At the end of the seventh, Rube Furber had struck out ten Carlton hitters. In the fourth, Kevlow had been handcuffed by a hard smash and had let a runner get on. The next Colt had sacrificed the man to second with a drag bunt, and Portsmouth's only .300 hitter had singled him home. Mose Watson had allowed but four hits.

The Braves came up in the last of the eighth still looking for a score. Sheckard led off after a short conference with Kelso. He took a ball, swung at a fast ball and missed, and Johnny Gramner, kneeling in the slot, watched Furber closely. Rube was as green as he was and had lots to learn, like not to telegraph his change of pace by a small grin around his wide mouth. He had it now. He fired it in and fooled Sheckard with the second strike.

Kelso called Cy away from the plate. When he went back he took a long chance and bunted on third strike. The ball rolled fair halfway between the third-base line and the pitcher's box. Sheckard beat Furber's throw by a step and a man was on.

The crowd was yelling for a rally. Johnny Gramner worked the speedball pitcher to a two-and-two count, and then he watched Rube's face as he peered at his backstop. It came in as expected, that one with the string pulling it back, and the rookie from Bridge City timed it and swung as hard as he'd ever swung in his life. The ball sailed high and far to left field and just dropped over the fence for a home run. The racket was deafening as he followed Cy Sheckard over the plate. Trotting to the dugout, he looked back at the Colt pitcher. "Tough luck, hayseed," he said.

The Braves looked at Johnny Gramner with admiration, even though they were not taking him to their hearts, not yet. Kelso said, "Good wallop, Johnny. It's a tough one for that kid to lose."

"He's a good boy," Mose said. "He's takin' it good."

"We'll belt him out the next time," Johnny said. "That shook him up."

Furber struck Hank Rawson out.

The Colts tied it in the top of the ninth. With one out, the Portsmouth center fielder caught one of Mose's hooks and drove it to deep right for a triple. Kelso ordered Mose to put the next man on to set up the possible double play. The pitcher worked carefully on the Colts' third baseman and got himself into the three-and-two count.

57

His next pitch was skied, not too deep, to Cy Sheckard, and Kelso knew what Cy would do. The Colts needed that run to tie. The third baseman would tag up and streak for the plate, and he was not a fast man.

The Portsmouth base runner on first also figured Kelso's way and started for the second sack. Cy Sheckard fired a bullet shot to Johnny Gramner on second instead of firing to Ox Janosky, but the rookie from Bridge City was looking at the man running home. The ball sailed by him, and Ox Janosky, watching the play every second, sprinted toward the Braves' dugout and stopped the throw from going in. He whirled and fired to third and caught the base runner sliding in. He walked to the dugout and threw his mitt against the old water cooler. "Tell that fresh rookie about a cutoff play, Dan."

Johnny Gramner took his place on the bench, his ears burning. "The runner could have been caught at the plate," he suddenly snapped at Sheckard.

Kelso said, "Get one any way you can," to Ox Janosky.

The big catcher hit at a three-and-one pitch and rolled weakly to the Colt first baseman. The rookie pitcher bowed his neck and struck out Long Sam and Irv Kevlow. The Carlton manager said, "Yeah, that home run shook him up," and some of the players laughed as they took the field.

The game went into the eleventh, and when the Colts got a man on, their manager sent in a hitter to bat for the pitcher. The freckled rookie was halfway out to the plate when his manager called him back. The noise from the fans built up until it was like the roar of Niagara as Rube Furber returned to the dugout.

"A great kid," Kelso said to Leo Masi. "He'll win a lot of ball games."

Mose Watson's third pitch to the pinch batter was

drilled right at Flit Buhel in left, and the old hurler struck out the Colt lead-off man. A left-hander took the mound for the Colts, and Johnny Gramner, first up in the inning, singled off the third baseman's glove. The crowd forgot the Portsmouth pitcher and concentrated on their own prize rookie. The stands were rocking, and Kelso hoped the old wreck would not collapse.

Hank Rawson drove one deep to the Colt shortstop, and the player knocked it down, picked it up, and fired to second. Johnny slid in and dumped the Portsmouth keystone man, and all hands were safe. Ox Janosky took a called strike and singled deep to center, sending Johnny around with the winning run.

The rampaging Braves had it easy in the windup, shelling four Colt pitchers for seventeen hits and ten runs. Whitey DeLong pitched an eight-hitter, allowing but one run, and Johnny Gramner belted three singles.

In the locker room, the word came that the Laraine Robins had won one from the Wooster Buckeyes. "Another half game picked up," Kelso grinned. "You'll pitch against Freeport tomorrow night, Hooks."

Long Sam Aber was still talking about his circuit clout in the first inning of the nightcap. "After seein' that Furber, Kelso," he said, "that left-hander was throwin' melons at me."

"That boy is a pitcher," the Carlton manager said. "Seventeen strike-outs! Johnny, you and he will meet some day in the majors."

"I'll make him my cousin," Johnny said.

It rained the next day and washed out the last of the three-game series. A letter arrived from Johnny's mother, and after he'd read it he took it over to Kelso's house six blocks away. He let the manager read how the police had picked up some of a Bridge City gang of youngsters for vandalism. Al Sava, his mother had written, had paid for the damage, and the boys, pals of Rick's, had been let go after a stern lecture from the judge.

"So Sava's no good, huh?" Johnny said. "He stands behind those kids, Mr. Kelso. You've been wrong about him all along."

"Maybe," the manager said. "I still think he's no good. Maybe you'll get a bill from him, Johnny, one way or another. What have you heard from your brother, Rick?"

"I never write letters," the second baseman said. "Let the kid take care of himself like I did."

Kelso got up and walked the floor, keeping his eyes on Johnny Gramner. "You realize what you could do for all those kids on West Lancey in Bridge City? You could go back there and show them a guy who made good, that a man has as much chance in the world as another if he wants to play it right. They want to see a hero, Johnny, not just hear about one. Wear that new suit you bought in Logansville and go down there on an off day."

"I don't want to see that dump again, Kelso. The smells make me sick. When I've got dough enough, I'll build my mother a house in the country." Johnny headed for the door. "And pay Al Sava back."

"That I'm sure of, Gramner," Dan Kelso said sourly. "And I hope it won't be with your future."

At ten o'clock the next morning, Johnny Gramner walked into Latham's office. Latham put a newspaper aside and grinned at his star second baseman. "I was just reading about that double-header yesterday, Johnny. Reads very good."

"That's why I'm here, Mr. Latham." Johnny sat down near the man's desk. "I want more money."

Latham sighed and leaned back in his chair. "Just like that, Gramner. A demand."

"The stands were packed on Saturday," the second baseman said. "They'll be that way most of the time when we're home."

Latham nodded. "And we are still in the red for many days when they weren't, Johnny, but you wouldn't be interested in that. You have me over a barrel and you know it. I know it. What do you want?"

"Seventy-five every week."

"All right, Johnny. But that's the limit for the rest of the season, is that clear?"

Johnny thought for a moment. "That's O.K. with me," he said.

"We'll leave the contract as it stands, Gramner," Latham said. "The extra will go to you as a bonus."

"Thanks," Johnny said. He grinned at a stenographer and went out. If Latham wanted to save his bush league club, he'd have to keep his rookie happy.

Johnny was conscious of his power, and his walk assumed something of a strut as he went down Carlton's main business street. People kept saying, "Hello, Johnny." "Nice goin', Johnny." "Hi, flash," "Stengel send for you yet?"

It was good. In the old days it was, "Beat it, punk!" "Was it you stole that auto tire, Johnny?" "Git on home before I run you in, Johnny."

Sure, Kelso, I should go back and show the cops my new suit and laugh over the old days. Maybe the judge in the juvenile court wants my autograph. Kelso, you should be a probation officer, not a manager of a ball club.

He walked into a haberdashery and bought himself a

dark straw hat with a canary yellow band. He wore it at a rakish angle when he walked into Mrs. Grady's. The Carlton rooter was checking the keys in her little cubicle in the corner of the lobby. "Well, aren't you the one?" she greeted the rookie. "Say, that was a dumb play you made last Saturday. Sheckard had the cutoff play down to a T, and you stood there like a chump and let his throw go by. It would have been a double play without a run scoring."

"Sure, I'm a chump." Johnny grinned. "A big one, and I just nicked Latham for more dough for bein' one."

Mrs. Grady eyed her roomer as only she knew how. "Well, well, then you can afford to pay me five dollars more per week, Mr. Gramner."

"Now look—"

"You look. The rates here are low enough, and I make them that way for most of Dan's boys," Mrs. Grady said. "When they can afford more, they—Johnny, didn't you tell Kelso baseball was a business?"

"O.K.," Johnny snapped. "Then maybe I can get fresh towels from now on."

"Sure. For a fresh ballplayer." Mrs. Grady grinned. "Wise up, sonny. You're not as tough as you make out. If you belonged to me I'd box your ears and put you to bed without any supper."

He could not find an answer for Mrs. Grady. Talking back to his mother had been easy, but this woman could deflate his ego with a look or a word. As he went up the stairs Mrs. Grady called after him, "And that was a fluke homer you got off that Colt pitcher. The wind blew it out of the park, Gramner."

His room was lonesome. Flit Buhel, who roomed with him, was in the country fishing with Long Sam and Ox.

62

It was great relaxation for any man, Long Sam always said, whether you caught anything or not. Johnny had never had a pole in his hands, so wouldn't know.

Later, when he was in the lobby asking if a letter had come for him, Long Sam and Ox came in with a little boy about seven years old. He was wide-eyed when Long Sam said, "That's Johnny Gramner, Buster. Ask him."

The boy wanted an autograph on an old score card he must have found in some rubbish. When he had it and had gone out with a wide grin, the rookie said, "Guess he sure would like to be me."

Long Sam Aber nodded. "Yeah. When you get time, Johnny, sit down and think that over."

CHAPTER 6

IN MID-AUGUST, WITH ONLY NINETEEN GAMES LEFT to play, the Carlton Braves were just one game out of first place:

	W.	L.	Pct.
Laraine	46	29	.613
CARLTON	45	30	.600
Logansville	41	34	.547
Portsmouth	34	41	.453
Freeport	31	44	.413
Wooster	26	49	.347

The hottest team in the league, the Portsmouth Colts, came into Carlton for two night games the day it was rumored that a scout from the Class AA league club, Zanesport, was in town. Its parent club was the Philly Quakers, and it was on its way to a pennant for the first time in ten years. The Carlton *Advertiser* reported that Zanesport was after a utility infielder and a pitcher. When Dan Kelso read Matt Yager's column two hours before game time, he began to feel jittery. The scout could be in Carlton for just one reason, to look at Johnny Gramner. Or, he hoped forlornly, it could be Rube Furber, the leading pitcher in this minor league. The farmer boy was due to start tonight.

Over the long pull Gramner was hitting .341, and his fielding had improved. As Yager said, he was certainly the best infielder in the league, if not the most popular among the players. Johnny Gramner played the game for all it was worth, the sportswriter said, letting the readers interpret his meaning as they wished. He had a heart covered with rawhide, Long Sam Aber contended, with regulation stitches. Fans resented the wall of reserve he had built around him, much stronger than Farrington Park's splintery center-field fence.

Dan Kelso was trying to make up his mind about his starting pitcher when his wife called him to the phone. "It's Mrs. Grady," she said.

"Dan," the ardent Carlton rooter said, "can you drop over here? I've got something you should see."

The manager hurried to the hotel, and Mrs. Grady led him up to Johnny Gramner's room. "He went to the movies, Dan, and I came up with fresh towels. I found this letter on the floor and couldn't help reading it." She shook her head. "I don't like it, Dan."

Kelso picked up the letter. Quickly he read:

64

"Dear Al:

Thanks for the letter. If I were you I'd wait a couple of days before you decided we are set to win the pennant. I can't tell you why, but maybe you'll find out for yourself before long. Anyway, hold up until you hear from me. Glad things are good with you, and you've put in another alley. Tell Ma I'm sending her. . . ."

"I wasn't snooping around, Dan," Mrs. Grady said. "I came to tidy the room up and couldn't help seeing it. What do you think he's up to?"

"Right now it could mean not a thing," Kelso said, but knew he was not fooling Mrs. Grady. "One thing I will stake my life on, though. Johnny Gramner would never throw a ball game."

"Then why?"

"Forget this, Mrs. Grady. Give me your solemn word you won't mention it to a living soul."

"May I be struck as dead as a pop fly, Dan," Mrs. Grady said.

Kelso made no mention of visting ivory hunters in the locker room at Farrington Park, but he was aware of the excitement in Johnny Gramner as the second baseman suited up. The stands were filled with more than two thousand fans once more. It was to be Old Mose Watson against the fireballer, Furber. The farmer boy had won ten games and lost one since coming to the Colts.

Mose started off shakily. He walked the first man up. The next batter lifted a long fly to left field, but Portsmouth's first baseman, Bolweig, doubled off the scoreboard in right. Cy Sheckard's fine throw in held the Colt base runner at third. Two were on and the Colt cleanup hitter was waving his bat menacingly at Mose Watson.

In the bull pen, Tony Rocca started throwing for Kelso.

McTigue, the batter, caught Watson's first delivery solidly and the ball screamed toward right field. The runners were going when Johnny Gramner made a diving catch that brought the fans off the seats. Olma ran to the second sack and Johnny, from a sitting position, fired the ball to him a few seconds ahead of the base-runner trying desperately to get back to the bag.

The applause lasted until Johnny had been in the dugout for fully a minute. If there was a scout in the stands, he had gotten an eyeful, Kelso thought. The manager went out to the third-base coaching box and called encouragement to Olma, leading off. Furber looked over the Braves hitter and then struck him out on four pitches. Sheckard, after fouling two off, popped to the Colt first baseman, and the crowd whooped it up when Gramner took his familiar stance at the plate, feet spread wide apart, the bat cocked high over his right shoulder.

Furber missed the plate on his first three pitches. Johnny looked at Kelso to get the sign. The take was on, so he let the Colt fireballer's perfect pitch go by and kicked up a little dirt. Again he watched Kelso, and grinned inside when he got the sign to hit the three-and-one if it was good. He studied Furber's face and saw that it was deadly serious. Rube pumped twice and threw and pulled the string. Johnny Gramner had timed his cut for the fast one and was thrown off balance. He missed the ball by a mile. Furber, he told himself, had been learning, too.

He got some dirt on his hands while Furber went to the rosin bag, his mind on the scout in the stands. In the batter's box again he swung at Furber's next pitch and fouled it back to the screen. He fouled off two more, and then the Colt pitcher threw one too low and Johnny trotted to first base.

Hank Rawson hit Furber's first pitch and skied deep to center. The crowd sat back for what looked like a pitchers' duel.

The Colts did nothing with Mose Watson in the top half of the second, and Furber struck out the side in Carlton's half. The goose eggs kept going up on the scoreboard until Portsmouth's turn at bat in the top of the ninth. The break came when Irv Kevlow overthrew first base after charging a slow roller from the Colt left fielder's bat. The runner went to second. Long Sam Aber and Kevlow came in for the bunt; Johnny Gramner moved into the hole and to the edge of the grass. The Colt batter dragged a bunt between the pitcher's mound and the third-base line, and Mose Watson pounced on it like a big cat and fired to third. The ball beat the base runner, but Irv Kevlow dropped it, making his second error of the inning.

Kelso came out to the box to steady Mose. Johnny and Long Sam came over, and the second baseman said, "He sure dug you in deep, Mose," and looked over at Kevlow.

"You feel bad. I feel bad, Johnny," the dusky hurler said. "How you think old Irv feel, huh? I'll get out of this somehow."

Old Mose stuck in there. The Portsmouth first baseman hit a three-and-two pitch that Flit Buhel ran in on and gloved not more than twenty feet behind the shortstop, and the Colt runner on third had to hold. Kelso waved his infield toward right when Mirandos, the Colts' Cuban catcher, stepped up to the plate. Mose threw a strike across, and then missed the corners with his next three pitches. Kelso ordered Mirandos put on, and the bags were loaded. The Colts' manager called his shortstop back from the plate and put in a pinch hitter, a powerfully built man with a bullneck and the arms of a blacksmith. Ten years ago Hack Neilson had caught for the New York Titans.

Old Mose slipped a strike across, and the crowd began to talk it up. Neilson let a curve go by, and the umpire called it a second strike. The racket from the stands built up. Hack hit the next pitch with the best part of his bat and the ball streaked toward Johnny Gramner. He lunged to his right, backhanded the ball, scooped it to Joey Olma, covering the middle bag, and Olma fired to Long Sam for the double play.

Old Mose waited for Johnny, fell in step with him on the way to the dugout. "You are a good boy, Johnny," he said.

The second baseman had his usual curt reply ready, but somehow he couldn't turn it loose. Writers around the circuit always said that if you didn't like Mose Watson there had to be something wrong with you.

"Thanks, Mose." Johnny felt a trifle sheepish. The stands were still shouting and whistling over the play. The Braves grinned at the second baseman when he ducked under the roof of the dugout. Kelso said, "So now let's get a couple of hits," and went out to the coach's box.

Johnny Gramner led off with the first hit off Furber since the sixth inning, and the crowd screamed for the rally. The Colt pitcher bore down and struck out Rawson and Janosky, and Aber grounded to short.

In the top of the tenth, the Colts' right fielder slammed Mose's first pitch over the center-field fence, and that

68

proved to be the ball game; the Braves were unable to score against Furber in the last half.

"Well, who has been beating that rube?" Kelso said in the locker room. "Sure, it was a tough one to lose, but we'll get that one back tomorrow night."

Johnny had to admit he was not suffering over the defeat. He had made two of the four hits against Furber and had held the score down with his fielding. He began to whistle as he dressed, and Kelso said, "Cut it, Gramner. We don't want a streak of bad luck. I remember when you hated to lose."

"Sorry," the ballplayer said. He hadn't lost. Maybe the team had. Superstition or luck? He'd never considered either as being contributory to success. You had it or you didn't. It was as simple as that in his book.

Carlton put an end to Portsmouth's seven-game winning streak the following night. The Braves knocked out the Colts' starting pitcher in the second inning and scored seven runs. Hooks Grozek coasted to a 14–4 win, and home runs were hit by Rawson, Aber, and Gramner. The second baseman got three hits. Freeport managed to beat the Robins, 6–5, and the Braves picked up the ground they had lost.

The news rocked Carlton three days later. Dan Kelso had been expecting it, but he still felt the shock. A front page headline in the *Advertiser* said: "ZANESPORT OFFERS BRAVES PLAYERS AND CASH FOR JOHNNY GRAMNER. Deal Said To Be in Making."

An hour after the papers hit the stands, Dan Kelso was called to Latham's office. He recognized one of the men sitting near the owner's big desk. He had played with him at Minneapolis—the Zanesport scout, Ed

Pennoyer. He offered the old ballplayer his hand and said, "So you're raiding us, Ed."

"It's a good deal, Dan. That kid deserves a better ball club," Pennoyer said.

Latham introduced the business representative from the Zanesport front office, then asked, "What do you think, Dan? Ten thousand and an infielder and an outfielder from their farm club."

"Look at it this way," Kelso said. "Our attendance goes back to seven and nine hundred every game, Mr. Latham. The cash is no inducement, you know that. Gramner is the gate."

"It's our best offer, Latham," the Zanesport man said. "Gramner could fold in a faster league. He's a gamble. There's an infielder in Beloit we can bring up if this falls through. We've already got Rube Furber from the Colts and that is the only deal we may need to insure a pennant. Well, you have twenty-four hours to think it over."

Latham looked at Kelso. The manager said, "We'll trade the pennant away, boss. Remember that."

Latham nodded. "One thing you have to consider, Dan. Gramner knows about this, and he'll have something to say about it. All right, Kennedy, I'll give you your answer this time tomorrow."

Dan Kelso left Latham's office and was stopped at the next corner by the Carlton second baseman. Johnny Gramner's eyes were bright. "They make the trade?" he asked.

"We've got to think it over," Kelso said. "There's more than just a ballplayer involved. We have the fans to think of. They've been looking for a pennant for a long time, Johnny."

70

"They have no right to keep me in this bush league town," Johnny told him. "Would they pension me off if I broke a leg in that crumby infield? They'll trade me or else!"

Kelso said, "I expected this. O.K., we'll see." He left Gramner standing there, knowing that the kid would be in a Zanesport suit in less than a week.

Hours later, after four innings had been played against the Logansville Blues, the Braves' prize second sacker had booted a double-play ball to lead to the scoring of three runs against Whitey DeLong. It was not intentional, Kelso knew. Gramner was thinking of the big step up the ladder, and he couldn't bring himself to blame the kid too much. Another young ballplayer could get there ahead of him, and he might never get another chance again. True, they could hold him to his contract, such as it was, but no dissatisfied player is an asset to any ball club.

When the Braves came off the field to bat in the last half of the sixth, four runs behind, Dan Kelso took Johnny by the arm. "You're looking pretty bad tonight, Gramner. Maybe that Zanesport scout will make some changes on his report if you don't snap out of it. They consider temperament in a ballplayer's diagnosis, too."

"You mean—?"

"Get yourself a hit," Dan Kelso said, and went out to third base.

In the coach's box, Kelso remembered ballplayers who'd had a blind sense of loyalty, but they'd had better beginnings than Johnny Gramner. How could you blame the boy for a certain amount of selfishness when a policy insuring him against having to go back to West Lancey Street was dropped in his lap? He looked into the stands and immediately recognized the protest against wrecking a pennant team. There were no more than seven hundred fans present. He cleared his mind and looked in at Whitey DeLong, leading off for Carlton. "Get hold of a good one, Whitey," he shouted.

The pitcher fanned and Olma drew a walk. Sheckard watched two go by, then hit one to his liking through the box and into center field. The fans applauded when Gramner dug in at the plate. "Don't let us down, Johnny!" a deep-voiced fan yelled.

Johnny Gramner stepped into the first pitch and sent the ball crashing against the wall in right center, and Olma and Sheckard scored on the triple. Johnny looked at Kelso as he stood on the hot corner, and grinned.

The manager said, "That's the right recipe, Johnny," and remembered the day he had been plucked out of an obscure league and dropped into a Class AA ball park. The circumstances had been different, the team he'd left had been close to the bottom and going nowhere. He'd had ambition, he admitted, but also his share of sentiment. He wished Johnny had a little more of that.

Hank Rawson belted a long fly that brought Johnny loping in for the third Carlton run, and then Ox Janosky, burned at the world in general because of the news going around, swung from his heels at the first pitch and drove it out of the ball park.

Logansville brought in a new pitcher. He struck Long Sam out, but the score was tied.

A resentful Carlton team kept swinging and connecting for the rest of the game and walked off the field with a 14–6 win.

Long Sam, peeling off in the dressing room, suddenly addressed the Braves. "We don't have to lie down and play dead because we're losing a hot ballplayer. We don't have to face that Rube Furber no more, and that Zanesport club will have to give the boss a real second baseman or there's no deal!"

Johnny Gramner sat on the bench, taking off his spiked shoes. He said, "Sure, you can win without me," and grinned down at the concrete floor. He'd have to write Al Sava when he got to Mrs. Grady's.

"That's the right talk, Sam," Kelso said. "We are getting two infielders, don't forget. We'll take those Robins."

Johnny's head came up slowly and he stared at the locker in front of him. A feeling he had never known had come over him. All at once the satisfaction of leaving this tacky ball park was not as strong as he thought it would be; he knew now that he wanted them all to wish him luck when he packed his glove and his shoes. He wanted to thank the players who had corrected his mistakes. Then he made himself think of the old days to get the softness out of him.

That night he wrote Sava a letter telling him the Braves were by no means a sure thing to win the pennant. Kelso's pitching staff was not steady. Grozek's arm was beginning to bother him, and Aber's knee was starting to fold. Kevlow played on a dime. The new men from the Zanesport club were not expected to be terrific. He took the letter down to Mrs. Grady's desk and put it with the other outgoing mail.

The deal was made the next day. Johnny Gramner was to report to the Zanesport club just after the two-game series with the Freeport club the last of the week. The fans protested the transaction through the newspaper, the

73

civic clubs, and a delegation that called on Latham threatening to boycott Farrington Park. But the papers had been signed.

Gramner, as Kelso anticipated, played under wraps against Freeport. He took no chances with the base runners at the keystone sack, missing two double plays in the first game. Razor-sharp spikes could ruin a man in a few seconds. There were not more than two hundred fans in the stands to watch Freeport beat Mose Watson, 4–3.

The next morning Johnny got a brief letter from Bridge City. Al Sava wrote that he'd bet a big bunch of dough on the Robins. Johnny shoved the letter into a dresser drawer and looked over his wardrobe. He had four suits now and as many pairs of shoes. He picked out his light blue to send to the cleaners. In forty-eight hours he'd be packing.

The Braves beat Freeport, 10–8, in Johnny's last game. When it was over and the team was in the locker room, Mose Watson said, "Johnny, we all wish you luck where you're goin'. It'll be a tougher league, but we guess you'll stick O.K." He held out his hand.

"Thanks," Johnny said. "I guess you guys won't miss me much. I, well, I never knew how to mix very well." He felt a lump in his throat and waited until it cleared. "Seems I'm a heel for leaving Carlton—but, a guy has to look out for himself. Well, I hope you win the pennant."

Kelso said, "I'll see you before you go, Johnny."

Johnny left for Zanesport by bus late the next afternoon. When Mrs. Grady cleaned his dresser out for one of the new players, she found his last letter from Al Sava. She put it in the pocket of her apron, intending to forward it to Johnny, and went on with her work.

74

AN HOUR OUT OF CARLTON, JOHNNY GRAMNER LAID aside the magazine he was reading. He couldn't concentrate; it failed to get his mind off the players who would be suiting up in less than two hours in the dressing room at Farrington Park. He had been certain he could take this transition in stride and that those bush leaguers had merely been so many names. He found himself thinking of Dan Kelso and remembering the soft voice of Mose Watson, encouraging, mildly critical, and exciting laughter. The others, too. All of them had helped him in many little ways. Then he reminded himself that helping him had been to their advantage. Maybe Kelso would get a cut out of the Zanesport deal. Deliberately he put the Braves players out of his mind and thought of Al Sava, and the hardness appeared around his mouth once more.

When the bus stopped at a place called Hazelton, Johnny got off and went into the drugstore for a cold drink. Afterward he bought a newspaper and went back to the bus, where he found a girl occupying his seat and reading the magazine he'd left there. He stood looking at her, his impatience short-lived. She wore a dark-blue dress and a little white hat perched on the back of her head. Her hair was light brown and she had eyes to match; her small full-lipped mouth was brightened by a minimum of lipstick. Suddenly she became aware of his scrutiny and put the magazine down. "Oh, is this your seat? I'm so sorry."

As she started to rise Johnny said, "It's all right. Stay put," and took the aisle seat.

She thanked him and opened her bag to take out a compact. Johnny tried not to steal a glance at her, but the temptation was too great. All other girls he had met, and they'd been few, had been *dames* in his mind, and he had simply been tolerant of their existence. This girl was the kind he'd seen in the movies but never believed existed. His heart beat faster than it had the last time he had circled the bases, and this annoyed him for a moment. He looked at her out of the corner of his eye once more. She was tucking little loose strands of hair in place, the mirror tilted at an angle that caught Johnny's reflection. She looked at him briefly, snapped the compact shut, and turned her glance toward the scenery rushing past outside.

Three miles later, Johnny Gramner summoned all his courage. "Maybe you'd like to read some of the newspaper? It's kind of tiresome just looking out the window."

"Thank you." The girl gave him the sweetest smile he'd ever seen. She accepted the first section of the paper and scanned the headlines. Johnny studied the sports page, looking for a certain bit of news. Finally he saw his name in a column under a syndicated sports cartoon: "*. . . and the Zanesport Tanagers bought Johnny Gramner from the Carlton Braves to bolster up their infield for the pennant drive. . . .*"

"Are you going to Zanesport?" Johnny finally asked the brown-eyed girl.

She turned her smile toward him and nodded.

"Me, too." He had to find out if she could be impressed.

He pointed to his name, then handed her the sports page. "I'm Johnny Gramner."

Her eyes widened a little. A few moments later she handed the paper back. "It must be exciting to be a professional baseball player."

"Oh, I don't know," Johnny said. "It's all according to how big the league is you play in, how good you are. The better player, the higher salary."

The girl's smile faded. She said, "Oh?" and looked out the window again.

"It's a business like anything else," Johnny went on. "You ever know any baseball players?"

"I must say I have," the girl said, and brought her eyes back to Johnny. "You've heard of Mel Wessler?"

"The first baseman on the Philly Quakers?" Johnny asked. "Who hasn't?"

"I'm his sister." The girl gave Johnny a different kind of smile that took a lot of starch out of him. "Mel would rather play ball than eat. He played through the last series with Boston with a spiked ankle. He's more than a professional ball player. He's an old pro. There's a difference."

Johnny, deflated more than he cared to admit, said, "You talk like a man I know. Dan Kelso."

"I've heard of him," the girl said. "If he's your friend, you're lucky." She picked up the newspaper again, turned the pages. Johnny sat back in his seat, his pride ruffled. Finally the girl said, "The reviewers really tear Bramfield's latest book apart. Have you read it, Mr. Gramner?"

"Huh?" Johnny grunted. "Who's Bramfield?"

The girl glanced at him, her lips tightening. "Well, he isn't leading the majors in hitting." She handed him the newspaper, leaned back in her seat, and closed her eyes.

Johnny Gramner thought, I'll stay in my place, Miss Snooty. Like always I'll look out for myself. He looked at the initials on her bag, M.J.W., wondering what her first name was, and how big he'd have to get to call her Mary or Mildred or whatever it was.

At Zanesport, he helped her to the platform. "Good luck," she said. "The Tanagers need all you've got."

"Maybe if you live here, we could—" The words scared Johnny and his throat tightened up.

"I'll be very busy," she said hurriedly. "I'm a nurse at the hospital. Thank you for making my trip shorter." She walked away and Johnny stood staring after her, not sure of what had happened to him. His heart had never been involved with anything but getting ahead in baseball. Picking up his bag, he hurried through the waiting room and into the street. A taxi pulled up and he ducked inside. "Fairmount Hotel," he said. The single players stayed there when the Tanagers played their home games. The married men had apartments or houses in or on the outskirts of the manufacturing town.

The taxi driver studied Johnny's face in the rearview mirror. "Ain't you that rookie, Gramner?" he asked. "Your picture was in the paper this mornin'."

"That's right."

"You'll like it here. It's a good baseball town," the driver said, and turned on the radio.

"—and that's a full count on Ebling. The Tanager infield has gone back now, figuring the bunt sign is off. DelGardo winds up and throws—it's a hot one straight to Armitage. He scoops it to Old Mitch at second, forcing —no, he dropped the ball—" A roar from the crowd drowned out the announcer's words.

The cab driver said, "That's why you're here, Gramner."

"—Two on now and only one out. The Lakers are leading three to one—"

The driver tuned the radio down. "Old Mitch Fenner is forty if he's a day. He's been playin' all year on a dime."

"Lot of 'em never know when to quit," Johnny said. "A smart guy walks out when he's ahead."

"Yeah," the driver said, and pulled up in front of a small hotel a few blocks from the residential section. Johnny paid his fare and entered the lobby. He heard the account of the night game coming over a radio. He asked the man at the desk if there was a room for Johnny Gramner, and the clerk looked at him for a moment, then grinned. "There sure is. And room in that Tanager infield. The Lakers are hammering us five to one." He checked the cards in the rack behind him. "Furber is due in tonight, too. That pitcher, Gramner—"

"I've met him." Johnny grinned and took the key the clerk slid toward him.

"You're rooming with Stan Coveskie," the clerk said. "The Tanager southpaw. You'll find him a nice guy."

Johnny picked up his bag and the clerk, watching him enter the elevator, decided to reserve judgment. The horsehide grapevine had hinted that the new second sacker was anything but a shrinking violet.

Johnny Gramner surveyed Room 78 briefly, found it an improvement over Mrs. Grady's rooming house, and peeled off his clothes to take a shower. Freshened, he pulled on a new bathrobe and lay down on the bed near the window. He saw a small radio on the table between the two beds and reached over and snapped it on.

"—that's the third out and the Tanagers come in for the last half of the fifth trailing by seven big runs. Folks, if you want a real ice cream, try Garden's new butter pecan. Always wholesome, always fresh. Mitch Fenner is coming up to hit. It's been a long night for the veteran. Two errors and struck out twice. Well, the new sensation from Carlton is supposed to arrive tonight. Maybe the fans will get a look at the rookie in tomorrow afternoon's game. Mike Gaffney is counting on him to fill the weakness at the keystone sack. Here's Fenner up. The first pitch gets the inside corner for a strike. That Laker pitcher is shaving the plate tonight. Four men have been caught looking so far—"

Johnny snapped the radio off, pillowed his head in his arms, and stared at the ceiling. So far, so good, he thought. He'd come up faster in one year than most rookies did in three. He was stepping into another old man's shoes, and he could only be an improvement, despite the better brand of pitching in this league. It was hitting that kept a man in his job. Base knocks paid off; they made the fans forget the fielding averages.

He kept seeing that pretty face against the ceiling— and the doubt in those brown eyes. Sure, he thought, he was bush league to her in more ways than one, but if he met her again it would be on the plush seat of a Pullman and not on a bus going back to where he'd started. He turned off the light and fell asleep.

Close to midnight he was roused out of his sleep, and he sat up and blinked at the slim, dark-featured man who was pulling off his shirt. "Sorry I woke you up, Gramner," the man said. "I'm Stan Coveski. We had a rough night. We lost eleven to five."

80

"Yeah?" Johnny turned over and dug his face into the pillow. "Maybe I came just in time."

Coveskie's usually placid countenance clouded a little. "Sure, we all prayed for your safe arrival, Gramner," he said. "I'll call Gaffney an' let him know or he won't sleep a wink." He grinned to himself and went into the bathroom, looking forward to the busher's welcome in the Tanager dressing room the next afternoon.

Ed Pennoyer came into the dining room when Johnny was having his breakfast. Five other Tanager players were at a big table on the other side of the room, and after he'd shaken the new arrival's hand Pennoyer said, "This won't do, Gramner. You're on this team. Come on over and I'll introduce you to those monkeys."

Coveski called out, "We invited him, Ed. He's bashful."

Johnny reluctantly followed Pennoyer to the big table. The scout introduced him to the Tanager first baseman, Ted Robek; a utility infielder, Flit Carrido; a left-handed relief hurler named Preacher Marcum; and the Tanager right fielder, Leo Kleiner. Coveskie said dryly, "We've already met, Ed."

Preacher Marcum eyed Johnny critically. "Hope you can stick, kid," he said. "We'll help you all we can."

"Sure," Johnny said. "If I need it."

Carrido looked at Leo Kleiner and shrugged. Johnny said to Pennoyer, "When do I meet Gaffney?"

"In an hour at the club's offices," the scout said. "There'll be some writers there, so don't give 'em stuff they can twist around, Johnny. They can club you."

"I don't care what they write," the fielder from Carlton said, "as long as it isn't my contract." He walked back to

81

his table and poured himself another cup of coffee, thinking along the wrong lines again, and making his first error by assuming that these players were patronizing him.

When he met Gaffney at the Zanesport business office, Johnny knew this man would be more exacting than Dan Kelso. He was big and broad-shouldered, with a weathered face and countless crow's-feet around eyes that had squinted at hundreds of towering pop-ups. He'd caught for the Chicago Bruins for six years. But he tempered his strictness with a rare sense of humor that had made him famous in organized baseball. He could handle men, knew how to separate them from the boys.

"You look fine, Johnny," the manager said. "I think you'll stick here."

Johnny nodded. "If the pay is right," he said. "It's O.K. for the rest of this year, but if I produce—"

Gaffney said, "You shouldn't be so hungry for one so young, Johnny." He eyed the rookie with less of a smile. "Let's wait until next year." He walked toward the door and opened it, called out, "Come in, boys."

Three writers came in and Mike Gaffney introduced them to his new infielder. Johnny ignored most of the questions they fired at him. One of them said, "A junior prima donna. I'll make up my own story." He hurried out and nearly bowled over a fat little man carrying a camera. Gaffney said, "Tiny, get it over fast. Just a couple now, you hear?"

"Johnny," the fat man said, "spread your hands on the table—like this. The hands are what we want—the hands like Gehringer's. Then one holding a bat like you was goin' to bust this picture of a Lansing southpaw I'm holdin' up. Great stuff, hey Mike?"

82

Johnny Gramner grinned. Al Sava had always said to get pictures in the paper. They were worth ten thousand words. He gave Tiny Kaplan all his attention, and the writers looked at each other and shut their notebooks. One turned to Gaffney. "You no longer have troubles?"

Mike Gaffney watched Johnny strike the belligerent pose Tiny had requested. He hoped he'd live to see the day when a rookie with real humility arrived from somewhere. Well, if he could play ball—

"Do I play this afternoon, Mr. Gaffney?" Johnny asked when the pictures had been taken.

"You can call me Mike," Gaffney said, and shook his head. "I haven't made up my mind, Johnny. Maybe you'd better sit on the bench an' get used to the bigger crowd and have a close look at the brand of ball we play here. Believe me, kid, it'll be different."

"If you thought I wasn't ready," Johnny asked, "why did you bring me up here?"

Mike Gaffney looked at his new second baseman the way he looked at umpires when he thought they were doing him wrong. "Be at the ball park at twelve thirty, Gramner. As to your question, I was in a spot. I was desperate—thank fortune you play a short schedule in that bush league. I didn't have time to look around for better material."

Johnny said, "Yes, sir, Mr. Gaffney," and knew for sure this was not a Dan Kelso. He was even more certain that he'd better produce when expected, or he'd never see a major league park. Mike Gaffney was a baseball man, big in stature and reputation.

CHAPTER 8

GLOVE AND BASEBALL SHOES TUCKED UNDER HIS arm, Johnny identified himself at the gate of the Zanesport ball park, and the man in charge let him through and gave him directions to the home team's dressing room. More than a dozen players were sitting around when he walked in, one of them a short stocky man with traces of silver in his hair. Leo Kleiner nodded to the rookie and said, "Mitch, this is the guy taking over your spot. Johnny Gramner."

Middle age offered his hand to youth. "Nice to meet you, Johnny, and lots of luck. I've had twenty years of baseball and wouldn't swap it for all the rice in China." Mitch Fenner's face, toughened and bronzed by the sun, split into a genuine grin. "I've been up and down and all of it was good."

"I hope you've saved some money, Fenner," Johnny said.

The veteran glanced at the players around him, his brows lifting. "Don't you cry for me," Fenner said, still smiling. "I'm managing Racine in the Tri-State League next year. If you ever need a job, kid—"

Leo Kleiner, the Tanager's power hitter, enjoyed this. He said, "Gramner, hold him to that. You never know."

Players kept trickling in. After a while Johnny met them all, and then Gaffney came out of his little office and told his team to suit up. "Gramner, there's a uniform back from the cleaner's should fit you O.K. Take the locker next to Nick Stenji's. It's hanging up there."

Johnny's nerves were singing a little. The talk in this dressing room was bigger time. Half of these Tanager players had been in the majors and he remembered reading about them when he was in school. Chico Gonzales, utility infielder, had been with the Cleveland Redskins for nearly two years. Preacher Marcum, Gaffney's top fireman, had hurled for the Brooklyn Bums for six years. And there was Wally Felsch, the left fielder, who had been in a world series and had hit a homer against the Yanks. He felt good when a hand banged him on the shoulder. "Hi, Johnny. It's nice to be on the same ball club." He turned to look into the smiling countenance of Rube Furber, the pitcher up from Portsmouth.

"Right," Johnny said, and took his uniform off the hook. The shirt was piped with red and two scarlet birds perched on a limb across the front, just above the red script *Tanagers*. The stockings were red with two thin black stripes above the ankles. The visor of the cap and the button on top were also red.

"I may start today," Willie Furber said proudly. "Don't boot too many behind me, Johnny."

"I don't think I'll be in there," the second baseman said, and leaned over to pull on his shoes. The racket around him was the same as it had been in the smaller league dressing rooms. The smells were the same. Outside he knew he'd see a difference. The crowd would be bigger, the outfield more spacious, and that fence would seem miles away.

Gaffney barked, "Get the lead out. After those last two games you need some hitting practice."

85

Johnny stood up and looked around him, banging his fist into the palm of his old glove. Cass Whitlow, lead-off man and team captain, sat on the table while the Zanesport trainer tightly taped his ankle. Pat O'Dowd, the catcher, still bare from the waist up, was rubbing liniment into an ugly bruise on his shoulder. Rube Furber said to Johnny, "Let's go out and have a look."

The rookies followed four of the regulars to the home team's dugout, and Johnny's pulse quickened as he looked at the diamond. The grass seemed very green, the infield as smooth as a table top. This ball park was one of the best in the hinterland and represented quite an investment on the part of the Philadelphia Quakers, the Tanagers' parent team. The foul lines seemed miles long to Johnny. The center-field fence looked as if it might be in the next county and the stands, he had heard, could accommodate twelve thousand fans.

The Tanagers filled the dugout, chattering like a cage of monkeys. "All right," Gaffney said. "Break it up and grab those bats!" He singled out seven men, Johnny Gramner included, and sent them out to the field.

Cass Whitlow faced the batting-practice pitcher first. He cut at the second delivery and smashed it on the ground between first and second. Johnny raced into the hole, gloved it, and fired to Joe Narin, utility infielder, on first. Narin threw the ball toward the pitching mound. Johnny looked at the players around the batting cage, but none of them seemed impressed. He watched Whitlow hit a few more, then moved back when big Ted Robek stepped in for his cuts. Robek fouled one a mile high, then belted a fast ball over the roof of the right-field pavilion. He hit the fence with a drive that never

86

rose higher than ten feet, and skied high and far to the fly shagger in deep left center.

Gaffney had them hitting for nearly half an hour, and finally he sent Johnny Gramner in for his cuts. The Zanesport regulars watched with interest now. The practice pitcher looked at the rookie for a long moment, then glanced toward Mike Gaffney. He nodded at the manager's signal and fired a fast ball. Johnny let it go by. The next pitch was high and outside and he kept his bat on his shoulder. Then the curve came and he timed it right and drove it on a screaming line inside the third-base line.

"Nice belt," he heard a player say, and thought it was Robek.

Johnny kept swinging. He sent the player in left back to the fence for two of his long flys. Afterward, the manager called a player off the bench and motioned to his new second baseman. "Johnny, this is Sam Berman. He's made hitters out of a lot of ballplayers. Sam, he's your boy!"

Berman, Johnny judged, was as old as Mitch Fenner. But he was leaner than the veteran second baseman and his eyes were ten years younger. Johnny asked, "What did Gaffney mean you've made hitters out of—?"

Berman grinned. "Sure, you hit good in that bush league, Gramner. But you're facing better pitching here and playing a different brand of baseball. We play a lot of hit and run, and run and hit. There's times when a man has got t' know how to hit behind a runner. I've been watching you, Johnny, and you've got some things t' learn. One thing you must remember if you want to stay up here, and that's you can still learn in this game of baseball. Robek is our top hitter, but a month ago he went into a slump that nearly benched him. I got him squared around."

Johnny said, "O.K.," and turned to watch Gaffney's wizardry with the fungo bat.

"We'll begin early on Monday," Berman said. "A man's got to know how to hit to right field when the occasion demands it, Gramner. Too many hitters today are swingers, aimin' all the time for the fences."

After one o'clock the stands filled rapidly. Johnny, after infield practice, looked at the visitors' dugout where the Lansing Senators were milling around in their gray road uniforms. He had learned from the local sports pages that the Senators were now in third place, two and a half games behind the Tanagers. The Lake City Oilers were leading the league by only two games. The papers had said that Gramner and Furber could be the difference in the stretch, yet Gaffney was treating him as a Little Leaguer, and Berman apparently had never been told about his hitting with the Carlton Braves.

Later, Johnny watched the Lansing team take infield practice and grudgingly admitted this was a different brand of ball. The stands gave out with a steady roar now, and he was certain the crowd was well over six thousand. Mike Gaffney called Cass Whitlow over and gave him the Tanager batting order. In front of the third-base boxes, Furber was warming up along with Harde-man, a southpaw. Across the way, the Lansing pitcher, a man over six feet and weighing all of two hundred pounds, was loosening up. Johnny felt like a new kid in a strange school, and all at once he was a little afraid he might not meet with Gaffney's approval. Again he saw the doubt in a pair of soft brown eyes, and he rubbed the clammy palms of his hands across the letters

88

on his shirt. Someone sat down beside him and said, "You've got butterflies in your stomach, Johnny. They'll be gone once you get in the line-up."

It was Stan Coveskie. Johnny made no reply. The field was cleared now, and the fans turned loose a pre-game racket of impatience. Mike Gaffney went out of the dugout and conferred with the bull-pen catcher, Ray Mosser. The negro backstop nodded, and Mike walked over to Rube Furber.

Leo Kleiner said, "He's goin' to start that kid. He looks like he might do it."

Furber came into the dugout, and the veteran players gave him words of encouragement. "Don't try too hard, Rube," Pat O'Dowd told him. "You've got fielding behind you. Let us do some of the work."

Cass Whitlow went out to the plate with the batting order and to discuss the ground rules with the Senator playing manager. Cass came back in, picked up his glove, and led the team onto the field. Johnny's eyes were on the man starting at second base for the Tanagers, Chico Gonzales, and he grinned when he heard a voice in the stands yell, "Where's the busher?" There was a timbre of resentment in the roar of the stands, but Mike Gaffney gave no sign that he had heard. He sat a few feet away from Johnny, his arms folded, chewing slowly on his gum. His eyes were on his pitcher.

The lead-off man took Furber's first pitch for a strike, a fast ball that made a cracking sound in O'Dowd's big mitt, and the fans yelled. Furber's next pitch was low, and the Tanager catcher had to stop it with his body. Gaffney shifted his feet nervously when the rookie threw three more bad ones. Speck Armitage came in from short and steadied the farmer boy.

When Furber lost the next man on five pitches, Gaffney went out in front of the dugout and signaled to his bull pen. A right-hander got up and began throwing. The Lansing power hitters were coming up. Johnny Gramner heard the Senators on the bench begin to pour it on when Babe Darlman, a .349 hitter, took his stance at the plate. The jockeying back in the smaller league had been mild in comparison.

Darlman fouled one off, let two go by, then hit one deep to short that Armitage knocked down but could not throw. The bases were filled. Cass Whitlow called time and joined some of the other players on the mound. Mike Gaffney got up and went out to talk to the rookie, and Johnny said, "They ought to take him out."

"This is where he'll show his moxie, if he has it," Coveskie said.

The crowd booed when Gaffney walked back to the dugout, leaving Rube Furber in.

The rookie looked the cleanup man over, studied O'Dowd's sign. He cut loose and whipped a fast one by Eddie Jenke, the Senators' slugging center fielder. Jenke looked at the next one, a fast-breaking curve that got the outside corner. He watched a waste pitch go by, and then worked the count to three and two. Jenke did not look at the third-base coach. He was on his own.

Furber fired the fast ball and Jenke belted it toward Gonzales at second, who took it on a hop and fired into O'Dowd for the force at the plate. The Tanager infield moved back, anticipating the double play.

Rube Furber got ahead of the Senator first baseman with two called strikes, and now the fans were with him. O'Dowd signaled for a fast ball right down the middle, figuring the hitter would expect the rookie to fire that

90

waste pitch. The batter swung late and a lazy fly went up to the infield that Robek took without moving more than a couple of steps. The crowd, a lot of the pressure off, cut loose, and young Furber calmly went to the rosin bag and dried his pitching fingers. A hit could still score two runs, but a .267 hitter was up now. The Tanager infield talked it up, Chico Gonzales' broken English rising above the other voices. "Throw him een, amigo. We catch 'em!"

Furber worked himself into a full count against the Senator shortstop, then struck him out with a high fast ball. The Zanesport fans let bedlam loose as the rookie walked toward the dugout. Gaffney patted him on the back. "You'll never be in a tougher spot, Rube. Nice goin'!" He walked out to the third-base coaching box, and Chico Gonzales took his bat from the rack and headed for the plate. He was a good fielder, but a weak hitter. No man in the league, however, drew as many walks.

Chico got a base on balls after fouling three off, but Armitage hit into a double play. Ted Robek doubled off the right-field wall, but died there when Leo Kleiner flied deep to the Lansing right fielder.

Johnny watched the teams battle to a scoreless deadlock for six innings, marveling at some of the support given Rube Furber. Twice double plays had extricated him from ticklish situations, Chico Gonzales starting one that drew the crowd right out of the seats. Watching the Cuban, Johnny realized that he would have to earn that spot with his bat and not his glove.

In the eighth inning, after the Senators had scored a run on a walk, a sacrifice, and a bloop single to right, the Tanagers came in, the weak end of the batting order coming up. Wally Felsch, Gaffney's left fielder, hit a three-and-one pitch through the box for a single. The manager immediately went to his bench to hit for Rube Furber. George Rubeski went to the rack and picked a bat, and Johnny squirmed on the bench. Cass Whitlow looked at Mike halfway down the line, got the word, turned to Johnny and said, "You swing for Gonzales."

The announcer gave the fans the change through the loud-speaker. Rubeski let a low one go by, then dragged a bunt along the third-base line that he beat out by half a step. Johnny Gramner, a nervous lump in his throat, walked to the plate, and when his name boomed out of the speaker, the home town gave him a terrific ovation. Gaffney clapped his hands together. "Get hold of one, kid," he called out.

The southpaw in the gray suit glared at Johnny from the mound. He threw to first and nearly trapped Rubeski. Then he concentrated on the hitter. He threw a slider that caught the outside corner and Johnny looked down at Gaffney. The manager folded his arms and tugged at his cap. A fast ball, letter high, came in and the rookie from Carlton swung from the heels and slammed the ball straight at the Senator shortstop. He threw his bat away and ran half-heartedly to first. The double-play ball was in the dirt and the Lansing first baseman bobbled it, picked it up, and had the rookie out by a step. Fast running, every person in the park knew, would have spoiled the twin killing. A lot of the fans made Johnny Gramner know it as he went back to the dugout.

Cass Whitlow snapped, "We run them out here, Gramner. Gaffney will convince you."

Wally Felsch was on third, but there were two out. The Lansing pitcher reared back and struck Speck

Armitage out and the threat was gone. Johnny, on his way to the infield, got a taste of a big minor league crowd's displeasure. The faces of the players around him were grim. Preacher Marcum stood on the hill rubbing up the ball and looking at the one run for Lansing on the scoreboard. Johnny felt smaller than ever before in his life. The stands seemed gigantic, and the territory he was to cover the size of a cattle ranch. Trying to find an excuse for himself, he thought, A guy doesn't expect a player in this circuit to throw a double-play ball into the dirt. You were supposed to be nearly perfect.

Preacher Marcum cut the Lansing Senators down in order, and the Tanagers had one more chance. Johnny Gramner took his place on the bench, forgetting that he had thrown out the last Senator batsman on a routine play. It meant nothing when you'd already thrown it away.

With a slim one-run margin, the Lansing pitcher worked too carefully on Ted Robek and walked him. Leo Kleiner, swinging for the far barriers, struck out and the crowd groaned. It was Pat O'Dowd who swung on the first pitch and sent it high and far over the roof of the stands, just inside the foul line. When he came to the dugout with Robek, the entire Tanager team, with the exception of Johnny Gramner, gave him a hand. Misery, at this moment, desired no company. Johnny was just a guy sitting on a bench in a baseball suit. The fans had forgotten he was there as they swarmed to the runways, still talking about O'Dowd's circuit clout. The players moved into the runway under the stands to the dressing room, and Johnny trailed along with the bat

93

boy, a thin lad about twelve years old. Arnie Hagen had a leg crippled by polio and he couldn't walk too fast.

The bat boy said, "Forget it, Johnny. You'll make up for it. Gaffney gives a guy every chance."

Johnny shook his head and shouldered past Arnie, making no reply. In the dressing room he had no sooner slammed his glove down when Mike Gaffney called to him. He followed the manager into the little office. "O.K.," he said in a boyish pique. "I'm a flop. I nearly threw it away."

Gaffney cooled the player with a glance. "Get the chip off your shoulder, kid, and sit down!"

Johnny obeyed, his eyes on the floor.

"There's one thing I won't stand for on this ball club, Gramner," Mike roared. "Lack of hustle. Ballplayers are only human, and we consider an error now and then a part of the game. Loafing on the bases is not making an error. It's being as dumb as an ox, Gramner. It's crossing up a club that is close to a pennant. So on your first time at bat you don't hit a home run and you crawl to first base. Let me tell you one thing, sonny boy! Temperament and playing this game for yourself alone will send you back to the sticks so fast you won't ever believe you came up."

No, this was not Dan Kelso. It was Mike Gaffney, the man who could make you or break you. He's forgotten more about this game than you know right now, Johnny, so listen to the man!

"You saw that kid out there in the first inning, Gramner," Gaffney said. "The bases loaded and nobody out. The heavy hitters waving the sticks at him. He could have felt sorry for himself and thrown a gopher ball in, but instead he showed me all I need to know about him.

94

He'll go far, that Rube. You didn't expect us to have a red carpet laid out for you here? You earn a place on this ball club, Gramner, and you earn the respect of the players. Tonight you look at yourself in the mirror and talk to yourself." Mike took a cigar from a box on his desk and shoved it between his teeth. When Gaffney smoked a cigar he was not mad at a single person in the world. "That's all, Gramner."

"Yes, sir," Johnny said. He walked into the dressing room, and as he passed Pat O'Dowd, the catcher said, "Don't let it get you down, kid. There's always another day."

Stan Coveskie was nearly dressed. He came over to the rookie and grinned. "How about a movie tonight, Johnny? It'll get your mind off the first day."

"I've got things to do," Johnny said. "Some other time."

Back at the hotel Johnny found a letter from Al Sava that had been forwarded from Carlton. He went to a far corner of the lobby, ripped it open, hoping it would contain the medicine he needed at the moment. Al had written in his usual vein: *"Congratulations, kid! You're on your way. Saw your ma a couple of days ago and you'd be surprised at the difference that money you send her makes. Take it from me, keep swinging, or some guy will come along and the mgr will like his face, and you'll find the joker in your place if you boot a couple or get into a batting slump. They'll forget you are on the bench until some bush league team wants a guy and they'll ship you out faster than a case of spoiled codfish. Believe me, I've seen it many times. So stay on your toes.*

"The Braves won a squeaker yesterday. Old Mose. . . ."

Johnny shoved Sava's letter into his pocket, its familiar message hardly registering. She was a nurse at the hospital, she'd said. He went to the telephones and discovered Zanesport had two hospitals. He took a chance and called Union Hospital and asked for Miss Wessler. The woman at the board asked his name and then told him to wait. A few minutes later he was told, "Sorry, she's very busy, Mr. Gramner. It is impossible for her to come to the phone."

He left the booth, and went to his room. Oh, well, he thought, what reason would she have to remember a guy in a bus, anyhow?

CHAPTER 9

MIKE GAFFNEY KEPT HIS PRIZE ROOKIE ON THE bench for the greater part of the three-game series with the Lansing Senators. Johnny went in as a pinch hitter three times and failed to get a ball out of the infield. The Tanagers made it two out of three in the series, losing the last one by sloppy fielding. Chico Gonzales came up with two boots that Johnny knew he could have handled sitting in a wheel chair, and after the game the trainer discovered that the Cuban had been playing with a pulled muscle in his leg.

On the way to Des Moines for a swing around the western loop, Johnny read the sport page of the Zanesport *Herald,* and felt misgivings for the first time in his young life. The rookie, the writer said, hadn't shown much thus far. True, he had been given little opportunity and the fans would withhold judgment until Gaffney gave him a regular berth. Rube Furber looked like a great prospect.

Chico Gonzales would be out for several days, Charlie Agnew, the trainer, had announced that morning. Gaffney could use Flit Carrido, Johnny knew, but the veteran was only hitting .209. He consulted the standing of the clubs.

	W.	L.	Pct.
Lake City	66	50	.569
ZANESPORT	63	51	.553
Lansing	60	54	.527
Covington	59	56	.513
Topeka	56	57	.496
Omaha	54	60	.474
Youngstown	52	62	.456
Des Moines	46	68	.404

He threw the newspaper aside, and talk in the Pullman began to register. Cass Whitlow was telling Leo Kleiner and Nick Stenji about his two-year-old daughter and saying that the day he'd met his wife was the luckiest one he'd ever known.

"A man'll never get any place alone," Kleiner said. "Nick, you should marry that pretty cashier in the hotel in Topeka."

"I'm hittin' only two forty-eight, Leo. I couldn't support a wife on that figure." Stenji grinned. "But you're right. Even a cluck like me should have somethin' to fight for. Maybe if I did marry that girl, I could hit more curve balls."

97

Johnny looked at the flat topography of Illinois and could not get the girl he'd met in the bus out of his mind. He felt the same sort of frustration he'd experienced when he was eleven years old and had seen a shiny new bicycle in a store window. It had been a million miles beyond his reach. Why couldn't ballplayers just talk about baseball? He got up and walked toward the grill car.

Pat O'Dowd said, "Gramner won't ever meet anybody he'll like better than himself."

"Give him a chance," Stan Coveskie said, looking up from his magazine. "He's not quite grown up yet."

"Yeah," Leo Kleiner said. "You marry the right girl and there's nothing like it. Marry the wrong one—well, there's nothing like it. Who wants a game of bridge?"

The Tanagers arrived at the Des Moines ball park at seven o'clock the following night and got into their gray road suits. Gaffney conferred with Allie Renner, his pitching and first-base coach, in one corner of the dressing room for a few minutes, and then came over to Johnny. "You start at second base, Johnny," he said. "Have a good game."

"Thanks." Johnny's spirits soared. He even grinned at Ted Robek, the first baseman who was examining a spike wound in his leg.

Speck Armitage came over and said, "Check with me out there, Johnny, when there's men on the bases. We have to know who is goin' to cover where. Whatever you do, don't beef when they knock you over."

"I've taken it before," Johnny said.

"Not in this league." Armitage walked away.

Robek eyed Johnny askance. "Take Speck's advice,

98

kid. He's been around a long time. A new doctor listens to the old ones, no matter what school he went to."

There were no more than three thousand fans in the stands when the Tanagers' Whitlow took the batting order out to the plate. The Des Moines team had been in a slump and in the past three weeks had dropped from fifth to last. The Cubs were starting a left-hander against Gaffney's hitters, a fast baller who looked even faster under the arcs. Rube Furber, having finished his warmup, came in and sat next to Johnny. Speck Armitage was ready to lead off; Mike Gaffney had juggled his batting order for the Cubs. Johnny was batting seventh and regarded the position as anything but a compliment.

Speck went up to the plate and dug in. The Cub left-hander threw a fast one in and over, and the shortstop looked at Gaffney coaching at third. Again Speck looked and the umpire judged that the curve ball had nicked the inside corner. The Tanager hitter stepped out of the batter's box and glared at the man in blue.

The southpaw failed to make Speck bite at two wide ones, then tried to burn his fast one by. Speck hit it on a line to left field for a single, and Cass Whitlow stepped in.

The third baseman fouled the first pitch into the stands, then put the southpaw into a hole with a three-and-one count. Cass looked for Gaffney's signal, then watched the next pitch, which was too low. The fans began to clamor for a new pitcher when Ted Robek took his familiar stance, his legs spread wide, his bat lifted high. The Cub left-hander worked too carefully and walked him. The home club's manager walked to the mound and conferred with his catcher and two of his infielders, and when he left the pitcher in, the crowd got on him.

Leo Kleiner worked the count all the way, then skied deep to center. Armitage scored easily. Pat O'Dowd pulled one to right that missed being a homer by inches, then walked, and the bases were loaded again. Johnny Gramner, with Stenji up, knelt in the batter's circle, hoping the pitcher would stay in until he had his cut, but the Cubs' manager gave up on the southpaw and called in a right-hander from the bull pen.

Nick Stenji hit the new hurler's first pitch deep to the infield and was thrown out at first, a run scoring. It was up to Johnny Gramner to make this a big inning. He dried his moist palms with rosin before he stepped in. Back of third Mike Gaffney clapped his hands. "Get a good ball, Johnny."

The Des Moines bench began to needle the Tanager rookie. They asked him if he wanted the pitching mound moved up, and if it was true he'd hit .750 in the garbage-dump league. He let the first two pitches go by, swung at the third and missed. The right-hander made him wait too long and he stepped out of the batter's box and went to the rosin bag. He wished he could get the nervousness out of his legs.

After checking with Gaffney, he got in again, and the Des Moines pitcher threw him a curve he liked. He swung and felt the meat end of the bat hit the ball solidly. The crowd's roar told him it was fair down the left-field line, and Allie Renner, coaching at first, yelled, "Run for two, Johnny!" He went into second standing up, and had driven in two more runs. It felt like old times.

Wally Felsch caught the hitting fever and looped a single over second, and Johnny rounded third and scored the fifth run for the Tanagers. Furber went up to the plate and struck out on three pitched balls.

Rube set the Cubs down in order; the first three batters he faced popped up to the infield. Gaffney's second-place club scored another run in their half, with Robek lifting his twenty-fourth homer over the right-field scoreboard. Willie Furber stymied the Cub hitters for five innings, but got in trouble in the last of the sixth.

The Des Moines lead-off man, with a count of one strike and no balls, hit Furber's curve between Gramner and Robek. Robek and Johnny both went after the grounder, Robek missing it and Johnny gloving it at the edge of the outfield. Furber, however, failed to cover the bag, and the Cubs' hitter got a base hit. Des Moines tried the hit and run, but the batter banged one of Furber's slants high and deep to left, the man on first tagging up and going to second.

The Cubs' catcher worked Furber for three balls and no strikes, then singled to left field, the man on second going in to score. Speck Armitage, in position for a cutoff play, took the throw from Wally Felsch and fired to second, but the ball had to be retrieved by Ted Robek, for Johnny Gramner was not there. The Des Moines catcher reached second. Armitage walked over to Johnny. "Watch that play, kid. It can cost you."

Johnny Gramner found out that it could. The next batter singled to right, and a second run scored. Wes Noorvik, a .346 hitter, came up to the plate and hit a two-and-two pitch against the right-field fence. Mike Gaffney called time and strode to the mound. Armitage and O'Dowd met him on the hill, and Gramner kicked at the dirt. He had given the Cubs an extra run. Willie Furber said he was all right. When he was on the mound alone he turned and grinned at Johnny. "Like playin' against Logansport," he said. "Relax, Johnny."

The farmer boy reared back and threw his fast one, then a curve, and a change of pace, and got two strikes out of the three pitches. The batter tagged his next pitch, a screeching liner that was labeled a hit, but the crowd gasped when Johnny Gramner leaped high and snagged it in the webbing of his glove. He fired to Speck Armitage and caught the base runner off. Willie Furber waited for the second baseman and walked him to the dugout. "It evens up in the long run, Johnny," he said. "A boner, then a play like you just made. We got lots to learn about this inside baseball, I guess."

Johnny was leading off for the Tanagers. He hit the first ball for a single to short left, where the Des Moines fielder bobbled the ball, and he put on speed and headed for second. The crowd was up, knowing it would be close. Johnny hit the dirt and the Cub keystone man put the tag on him. The umpire called him out and he got to his feet, ripped off his cap and threw it out to the grass. The umpire thumbed him off the diamond, but Gaffney tore in and objected to the heave-ho.

In the dugout, Johnny snapped, "The robber!" He picked up his glove and started for the runway.

Pat O'Dowd said, "You were out a mile, Gramner. That umpire has been in this business for thirty years."

"Yeah?" Johnny whirled. "Then why is Gaffney beefin'?"

"For throwin' you out. He's tellin' O'Malley you're only a wet-eared kid, and that he should make allowances," Cass Whitlow said.

In the dressing room Johnny sat on the bench in front of the lockers and told himself that Gaffney couldn't

102

get sore for the two hits he'd made. He turned on a radio and slowly took off his Tanager uniform. When he was dressed, they were playing the seventh and the Tanagers were having another big inning. Flit Carrido, taking his place at second, hit a triple with the bases loaded, and Johnny felt insecure again.

The Tanagers came into the dressing room, Rube Furber grinning wide over his 12–3 win. Mike Gaffney eyed Johnny, his eyes storming. "Allie Renner told you to hold up at first, Gramner. That Des Moines fielder has the best arm in the league. Put those little things down in your notebook, and some day you might be a real ballplayer. That coach isn't out at first base posin' for the photographers, Gramner. And that little fit of temper will cost you just twenty-five dollars."

"I was safe," Johnny protested.

"You were out a mile!" Gaffney said. "And you slid into that base like a hippo with nine legs."

"O.K.," Johnny said. "O.K."

At midnight, in the hotel room, Johnny Gramner vented his spleen on Mike Gaffney, the umpires, and the world in general. He was feeling sorry for himself again, and declared he would get that twenty-five bucks back from the Tanagers a hundredfold. When he got in stride and started hitting and convinced Gaffney he was the only guy to play second base, he'd have the Tanagers over a barrel.

Stan Coveskie threw a magazine across the room and sat up straight in his bed. "I don't understand you. I'd play for Gaffney for just room and meals if I had to. You take for granted that everybody in the world is looking for the dollar bill. Listen, Johnny, I was in

103

Czechoslovakia when the Nazis came. They burned out my family, murdered my uncle and my sister. We didn't get out of that country until 1945, and then we were half starved. My mother died before she saw any kind of freedom. The G.I.'s in Heilbronn, Germany, taught me how to play baseball. I was thirteen years old, and they said every kid going to America should know how to play. A sergeant taught me how to pitch. Every day, when he had time, he showed me everything he knew about the game. He wasn't gettin' paid, Gramner. So you had a bad beginning! Mister, compared to thousands of other people, you were born filthy rich. You ought to do what I do every night. Get down on your knees and thank God you are living in this country, even if you're shipped out of this league tomorrow."

"O.K.," Johnny said. "Now sing the National anthem, and we'll go to bed."

"Johnny," Coveskie said, "you'll have to learn the hard way, I guess."

"I'll do all right," Johnny said, and snapped out the light.

In the dark, Stan's words echoed through Johnny's mind. Maybe, he thought briefly, he was a lucky guy—he'd never faced the kind of fears Stan had. And now he was really on the way up in baseball, headed for the majors. He'd made a lot of progress since the days when Sava got him his spot on the North Side Barons.

Then the thought of Sava thrust itself on him again. He could see the tough mentor of West Lancey Street, hear his harsh words of warning: "It's all business, kid. You got what they want, they take it. All this stuff about the great American sport is so much talk. Play it for money—that's what counts." Sava was right, Johnny told himself. Or was he? He wasn't ready to admit it yet, but the ghost of a doubt was flickering in Johnny's mind.

The Tanagers swept the Des Moines series and moved on to Omaha to play the Packers a double-header, twilight and night. Johnny Gramner's batting average climbed to .298, and his double in the last of the tenth in the getaway game with the Cubs won a 4–3 verdict for Preacher Marcum. In Omaha, Chico Gonzales was pronounced fit to play by the Tanager trainer, but Mike Gaffney decided to go with the rookie from Carlton. Zanesport started the Omaha stand only a game out of first place.

In the dressing room, Johnny knew he was beginning to belong and it felt good. He drew some of the team's good-natured ribbing. He'd been the first one there at four thirty, and Mike Gaffney had just come out of his office. He'd asked Johnny about his family.

"A mother and a brother," the ballplayer had said. "They still live in that crumby neighborhood."

"You're the lucky one," Mike had pointed out. "Baseball got you out of it. You've got a lot of talent, Johnny. You can earn enough to get them out."

Chico Gonzales slapped Johnny on the back. "You stop heeting so good. Chico maybe go back an' raise pineapples. *Quien sabe?*"

Johnny Gramner got three hits in the first game against the Omaha Packers. In the sixth he failed to cover first when Robek had charged in for a bunt, and Mike lectured him when he came to the dugout. "Sure, you're hitting the ball, Johnny. But you opened up a three-run inning for the Packers. Maybe you can drive in three

105

and make up for it. DelGardo is working his head off to get the hitters out. It's his bread and butter, too."

In the eighth, the Tanagers were trailing by a run. Pat O'Dowd opened the visitors' half with a single through the Omaha first baseman's legs. Nick Stenji, obeying orders, bunted down the first-base line, and O'Dowd went to second. Johnny Gramner dug in at the plate, worked the Omaha right-hander to a three-and-one count, then lined a clean hit over second to tie up the ball game. The Tanagers won it in the ninth with a Leo Kleiner round-tripper after two were out. Whitlow and Robek were aboard. Cass Whitlow limped as he came into the dugout. Charley Agnew caught him by the sleeve.

"Nothing, Charley," Whitlow said. "Turned my ankle rounding third. It'll be all right."

DelGardo retired the first batter in the last half of the ninth, but walked the second man. Omaha's shortstop smashed one down the left-field foul line, and Whitlow made a terrific backhand stop to hold the hit to a single, but he crumpled up on the base line and tossed the ball to Speck Armitage coming over. Mike Gaffney and the trainer came out, and half the Tanager team converged on the third baseman. Johnny Gramner looked at Whitlow's gray face, and thought of players like Pete Reiser of the Brooklyn team who had cut his career in half by making the old college try against the fences in the major leagues. A guy could have rocks in his head!

They helped Whitlow off the field and Flit Carrido came in to play the hot corner. Johnny felt the cold sweat come out on him. An injury and you could say you'd had it. A broken shoulder or a fractured leg could slow a man up years before his time and dump him back among the daily wage earners.

106

DelGardo, in trouble, bowed his neck and fired his fast one by the Omaha hitter for a strike. He threw a curve that failed to hit the corner and fired one that rolled past O'Dowd to the backstop. The base runners moved up. The man at the plate represented the tying run. The swarthy pitcher rubbed up the new ball and looked at his infield. Then he went back to work. He struck the Omaha hitter out, made the next one sky deep to Nick Stenji in center. The Tanagers went to the dressing room and learned that Cass Whitlow would be out for the rest of the season.

"The guy is nuts," Johnny said to Stan Coveskie. "Why didn't he sit out the rest of the game?"

"He's an old pro," the pitcher said. "I've seen him play a whale of a game with two bum legs."

"I don't get it," Johnny said.

"You will," Coveskie told him. "Or you'll never be called a pro."

Gaffney singled out Hardeman, the left-hander, and told him to warm up. "We want this game," he said to all. "The Lakers are idle today. A double win will put us even with them."

Two hours and a half later, the Tanagers picked up two runs in the top of the seventh and pulled ahead of the Packers by a single tally. When Johnny Gramner started out of the dugout, Gaffney called him back. "Sit it out," he said. "Chico, go in there." He called a utility outfielder off the bench and told him to take over for Wally Felsch in left. Johnny twisted his glove in his hands and scraped his spikes along the concrete at his feet. He'd made two hits and was out of the game. Gonzales was not hitting his weight.

In the last of the seventh, Johnny Gramner, still

grumbling to himself, watched Harry Carter, in for Felsch, throw out a runner trying to score from right on a fly ball. The throw was a rifle shot into O'Dowd's mitt, and the Omaha player was out by a foot.

Wally Felsch grinned. "I couldn't have got him in ten years. That, Gramner, is defensive baseball."

In the last of the ninth, with the Tanagers still holding the single-run lead, the Packers started a rally. Gaffney pulled Hardeman and sent in Preacher Marcum. There were men on first and second and only one out when Preacher faced one of Omaha's top hitters. Gaffney came to the edge of the dugout and signaled to O'Dowd. The Omaha base runner was taking a brazen lead off the middle sack when Preacher Marcum fired one wide. O'Dowd whipped the ball to second and Chico Gonzales was right there to take it. He put the ball on the Omaha base runner, and now there were two out and only one man on.

"Chico never misses on that play," Rubeski said. "You could have, Johnny."

"If you say so, it must be so." Johnny grinned at the concrete at his feet. Let Chico have his fielding. The fans remember the base hits. They pay off.

Preacher Marcum fanned the next batter with his baffling change of pace after the count went all the way, and the Tanagers collected their belongings and hurried out of the dugout. Mike Gaffney, on his way to the dressing room, caught up with Arnie, the bat boy, and put an arm around the lame boy's shoulder. "Stick with us, son," he said. "We're having a good streak. Keep putting medicine in those bats."

Gaffney hurried on ahead, and Johnny Gramner

108

touched Arnie on the shoulder. "Does Gaffney really believe that hokum?" he asked.

The bat boy looked straight at the Tanager rookie. "Maybe. It's part of the game."

Johnny laughed. "I'll buy me a rabbit's foot and a horseshoe tomorrow, Arnie."

"You'll probably need both," the bat boy told him, and limped to the dressing room.

CHAPTER 10

THE ZANESPORT CLUB CAME BACK TO THE HOME park in first place by a game and a half. The Tanager fans turned out to the tune of eight thousand fans to see Johnny Gramner, who had boosted his batting average to .309 on the road trip. The rookie knew he was the drawing card—the papers said so. Getting into his uniform this Saturday afternoon, he thought ahead to next year when his salary check should be very much bigger. He was no longer in awe of these top minor leaguers. True, Sam Berman and manager Mike Gaffney had given him the benefit of much of their baseball savvy, and Speck Armitage and Ted Robek had polished up his infield play, but that was their job. He still wondered from time to time if a certain brown-eyed girl had seen his pictures in the sports pages and had noticed that Johnny Gramner's name was now fifth in the batting order instead of seventh.

As he hung up his sport coat he felt the letter in the inside pocket. His mother had written to ask if he'd sent any money to Ricky lately. His brother always seemed to have money in his pocket, she said.

The kid has an angle, Johnny thought. Al is a good friend and is looking after him. More power to the little character.

Speck Armitage came over while Johnny was lacing his shoes. "I'm going out with a friend tonight, Johnny," the shortstop said. "She has a friend. I thought maybe we could double—"

"Yeah? Look, the other girl is always a squaw," Johnny said.

"Dora gave me her word," Speck said. "She said her friend was prettier than she was, and that's saying something, believe me."

"I don't know," the rookie said. "See me after the game."

Mike Gaffney started Poke Lundell against the fourth-place Covington Brownies, and was sorry fifteen minutes later. Lundell could not find the plate and walked the first two men. The third man up banged one deep to short, and Speck knocked it down but was unable to make a throw. Covington's Ray Shelly, a home-run threat, stepped up and belted a two-and-two pitch down the right-field line. Leo Kleiner played the carom off the fence beautifully, fired it to O'Dowd, and cut down the Brownie trying to score from first. O'Dowd rifled the ball to Flit Carrido at third and nailed Shelly sliding in. Two runs came over, but two were out.

Lundell worked the next Brownie to the full count, then threw his fast ball. The batter slammed it off Lundell's glove, and Johnny Gramner raced in, scooped

110

it up, and fired underhanded to Robek. The runner was out by a step and the crowd cheered as Johnny trotted to the dugout.

Hofer, the Brownie left-hander, had one of his best nights, and at the end of the sixth, had limited the Tanagers to three hits, one a double by Johnny Gramner. The Brownies put a scare into the partisan crowd in the top of the seventh when they loaded the bags on two walks and a drag bunt with only one man out. Felding, the Brownie left fielder, took a strike, watched two bad ones go by, then stepped into Lundell's slider and laced it deep to short. Speck Armitage dug it out, fired to Johnny Gramner, who just got the ball away to Robek before he was dumped heavily by the base runner coming in. The flash from Bridge City fell heavily and landed on his right side. He got up slowly, his right arm from wrist to shoulder feeling as if it had been hit by a heavy club. Fear was a cold lump in his chest.

Armitage, Lundell, and Robek ran over and asked anxiously how he was. Gaffney came out of the dugout, worried lines around his mouth, and the trainer hurried at his heels.

"Just shook up," Lundell said to the Tanager pilot. "He'll be O.K."

"Who got dumped, you or me?" Johnny flared up. He swung toward Gaffney. "The arm feels pretty bad, Mike."

Gaffney said, "All right, you're through for the night," and called Chico Gonzales off the bench.

A run had scored, and men were on first and third. Poke Lundell induced the next batter to pop out to Pat O'Dowd, and the Tanagers came in still on the short end of a 3–0 score.

Leo Kleiner led off for Gaffney and hit a three-and-nothing pitch to deep center, where the Covington fielder made a miraculous leaping catch. Chico Gonzales stepped in and struck out on four pitched balls. O'Dowd, in a batting slump the last few days, grounded out, short to first.

The game ended with Hofer striking out Wally Felsch and Sam Berman, the latter hitting for Lundell. Two men were left stranded and the home crowd moved toward the exits, making very little noise.

Gaffney asked Johnny how he felt when the Tanagers got to the dressing room, and the flash shook his head. "My arm weighs half a ton," he said.

Agnew had been rubbing the arm. He shook his head at Mike. "Nothin' broken, I'll swear to it," he said. "It ought to be all right by tomorrow afternoon."

Johnny was fixing his tie when Speck came up. "How about the date, Johnny?"

"Sure," the second baseman said. "But if she's a dud, I walk out. O.K.?"

"O.K." The shortstop grinned. "We call for them at six thirty."

"But we won't be through eating before—"

"Look, Sandy MacGramner," Speck said, "we're takin' them to dinner. Loosen up for once."

"O.K.," Johnny said. "But no steaks."

At the appointed time, Speck Armitage pushed the doorbell in an apartment house on Zanesport's west side. A blonde opened the door a few inches and peered out. "Oh, Speck!" she said, and swung the door wide. Johnny followed the shortstop into the small living room, feeling

112

all ears and all hands. Speck said, "This is Johnny Gramner, Dora."

"I've heard a lot about you," the girl said. "Make yourself comfortable and I'll see if Madge is ready. How did you make out today?" she asked Speck.

"We lost. Let's forget it." The shortstop grinned.

The girl went into the next room and Speck looked at Johnny. "A cute kid. Private secretary. Maybe I'll marry her."

"Why not stay happy?" Johnny sniffed. He picked up a magazine, idly flipped the pages, tossed it aside. "A highbrow, huh?" he said. "Can't we get out of this?"

"Go along for a while, Johnny," Speck said impatiently. "We——"

The door opened and Dora came out with Johnny's date. The second baseman looked into a pair of brown eyes and all at once the singing of heavy bus tires was in his ears, and the faint scent of perfume sent his heart hitting over .500. She was smiling at him, and as he got to his feet his legs were trembling.

"A surprise," Dora said. "Speck, they've met before. Johnny, this is Madge Wessler."

Madge said, "Hello, Johnny Gramner. How would you know Speck's girl was one of my best friends?"

"It's great to meet you again," Johnny blurted. "You know, I called you a couple of weeks ago. You——"

"I was on duty in surgery," the girl said. "I couldn't have talked to the President."

"Huh, I thought I was brushed off," the ballplayer said, and he felt ten feet tall and luckier than Gregory Peck.

"Let's get going," Speck said. "I'm starved. I could eat a left-handed pitcher."

113

"You didn't get fat off one today." Madge laughed.

They went to a small restaurant a few blocks away and had antipasto and scallopine and spumone. Speck took his girl out to the small dance floor and Johnny apologized to Madge. "I–I'm sorry. I never learned t' dance."

"It's all right." Her soft brown eyes studied him with interest.

"Funny," Johnny said, the old resentments stirring in him once more, "when you get somewhere everybody is your pal. You strike out a couple of times and they don't ask for your autograph at the gate. Make a couple of hits and everybody claims they know you."

Madge Wessler set her lips firmly. "Meaning that I came chasing you when you made some headlines in the newspapers?" she asked. "Look, Mr. Gramner, I've known ballplayers all my life. Big league players like my brother. They do not impress me. Is that clear?"

Johnny Gramner still was not convinced he had made an error here and he said, "Then why did you make this date with—?"

Madge Wessler slowly shook her head as she stared at the ballplayer. "You would never understand, Mr. Gramner," she said sharply. "If a dog wagged its tail when it met you, you would be suspicious that it was after your shinbone. Everybody who offers you a hand has to have an ulterior motive. A person who thinks that way must have a miserable opinion of himself, and I feel sorry for you."

"I'm doing O.K." Johnny stubbornly refused to believe that this girl, of all people, would be interested in himself alone. It couldn't happen to a guy who had come from West Lancey Street.

114

"Yes, in the box scores," the girl said.

"That's my business," Johnny said. "I'm a ballplayer. You're a nurse. We both work at our trade for the dough that's in it and look out for ourselves first. Period."

"I don't agree with you. No one gets very far in this world without considering others, without the help of the people around them." Madge looked up and forced a smile when Speck came back to the table with Dora.

"Well, what do you think of the blind date, Johnny?" the shortstop asked.

"I can't tell you which one of us is blind, Speck," Madge said, and picked up her purse. "I'm so sorry, but I've got one of those headaches coming on, Dora. You mind if we go home?"

An hour later, Speck Armitage and the Tanager second sacker strolled toward the Hotel Fairmount. "What happened while we were away from that table?" Speck asked.

"Forget it," Johnny said, knowing he had possibly made the biggest error of his life.

"Yeah," Speck said. "A mistake a lot of batters make. They stand with their bat on their shoulder and watch the good ones go by."

On Sunday Johnny reported to the ball park and told Mike Gaffney his arm was still bothering him and that he wanted another day's rest. The manager chewed furiously on his cigar and loudly regretted he had quit the garage business. Charley Agnew, massaging Robek's trick knee, looked at the second baseman, his eyes full of doubt.

"Well, let it happen all at once," Mike growled. "Arnie sick in bed with a virus, Cass Whitlow walking with a cane, and Preacher Marcum with a touch of lumbago."

The Tanagers' batting order had to be juggled again. Flit Carrido was in the number two spot in Whitlow's place, and Chico Gonzales, taking over for Johnny Gramner, was hitting seventh. O'Dowd was moved up to fifth position once more. Mike Gaffney sent DelGardo to the mound.

Johnny Gramner sat in the dugout and watched the Brownies knock DelGardo out in the first inning. Three runs were over when Gaffney signaled to the bull pen. Right-hander Billy Smith came in with two on and only one man out. Johnny wondered if Gaffney was blaming all this on the absence of the team's bat boy and mascot, Arnie Hagen, even though Carrido had made a bad error to start the ball game. Sure, they needed him there, but he had a good ten years left to play ball, everything considered, and not even a Zanesport pennant was worth aggravating a bruised arm.

Billy Smith got the Brownie hitter to bounce out to first, where Robek won the race for the bag. The runners moved up. A .237 hitter came up, and as is often the case in professional ball, the weak hitter will get hold of one. Billy Smith's second offering was powdered through the middle and two more runs came in.

The Tanagers battled back for six more frames, picking up two runs, and then the Covington Brownies fell on Billy Smith for three more runs in the eighth and pulled ahead by six runs. Mike Gaffney said to Johnny Gramner as he left the dugout for the coaching box, "If Armitage gets on, can you swing a bat?"

"Not too hard," the second baseman said. Gaffney stared at him for a moment, clamped his teeth together, and went on his way.

116

Speck hit a ground ball to the Brownie second base-man, who fumbled it and threw to first too late. Mike Gaffney clapped his hands loudly and called for action.

Flit Carrido stepped in and waited the Brownie right-hander out. He worked the count to three and two, fouled four straight pitches off, then strolled when the pitcher threw into the dirt. The crowd was roaring when Ted Robek stepped up. The big first baseman, long overdue, got hold of an inside pitch and drove it out of the ball park. The score was 8–5 now in favor of the Brownies.

Kleiner skied deep to right, and O'Dowd, still battling a slump, struck out. Nick Stenji took two called strikes, then singled through the Brownie first baseman's legs, and Gaffney gave his orders. Sam Berman said to Johnny, "Get a bat and hit for Chico."

The crowd raised the roof again when Johnny dug in at the plate. He watched a strike go by, looked at Gaffney, and saw the fire in the manager's eye. Gaffney signaled for him to try and get on. Rubeski was already in the batter's circle, waiting to hit for the pitcher.

The Brownie southpaw missed the corners on his next pitches, then broke off his curve. Another strike. Johnny looked over at Gaffney. The manager told him to swing. The ball came in, breaking away, but not too sharply. Johnny Gramner got set to take a big cut, suddenly relaxed and half swung at the pitch. The ball popped lazily to the Covington first baseman and the game was over.

Gaffney met Johnny halfway to the dugout. "That was a good cut you took. A Girl Scout could have swung harder. Listen, busher, every game counts in this pennant race. When I want a man to swing, I don't care if he breaks his leg or an arm doing it. Hits are scarce. Second basemen are on every limb. If I was sure you were gold bricking on me, I'd fire you all the way back to Carlton. Don't let me be sure!"

"I tried to take a full cut," Johnny alibied. "I felt a twinge in my shoulder."

"O.K., O.K.," Gaffney snapped. "So forget it."

Monday was an open day. The last game with the Brownies was under the lights on Tuesday night. Arnie Hagen was still sick in bed, and Ted Robek was on his way to Nebraska to attend the funeral of an uncle. Sam Berman would cover first base until he got back. Mike Gaffney glared at Johnny as the team suited up. "Could I prevail on you to try and play tonight, Gramner?"

Leo Kleiner laughed. Johnny said, his ears burning, "I'm O.K. The arm's all right now."

The Tanagers were certain, after the fourth inning, that they were deep in a slump. Mike started Stan Coveskie, who left in the third through no fault of his own. Two errors had cost him three runs. Hack Wejac, a little right-hander, took over and got the side out. The Brownies belted him out in the sixth. The scoreboard said Brownies 5, Tanagers 1, when the home team came up for their cuts in the last of the sixth.

Flit Carrido got brushed by a pitch and went to first, but Sam Berman forced him at second with a weak roller to short. The fans came alive when Leo Kleiner stepped in. The big hitter fouled one over the right-field pavilion, took a ball, then skied to center. Johnny Gramner, hitless for the night, swung on the Brownie pitcher's first offering and rode it to the right-field barrier for two bases. Berman scored from first and Johnny went to third on the throw-in, hitting the dirt and oversliding the bag. The hot corner man put the ball on him before he could scramble back in.

Hardeman stopped Covington for the next three innings, but the Tanagers still had three runs to make up. Johnny Gramner led off for the home team and got his second hit. He stood on first enjoying the cheers, mentally figuring his batting average, not particularly concerned with the score of the game.

Pat O'Dowd came out of his doldrums and singled to left, and now the Zanesport fans were on their feet, yelling for a garrison finish. Nick Stenji bunted the first pitch and advanced Johnny and O'Dowd, and Gaffney called on Rubeski to hit for Wally Felsch. The big Pole slammed one high and far to right that bounced off the scoreboard, and Johnny came in ahead of O'Dowd while the stands turned loose a crazy racket.

Gaffney went to his bench again. Narin, a utility infielder, came in to hit. He drove a pitch he liked to short left and Rubeski, running like a startled deer, rounded third and headed for the plate. The throw from the outfield was fast and true, and Rubeski was out. Mike Gaffney kicked at the turf when Speck Armitage dug in. He left the field a few moments later growling when Speck fouled out to the catcher. Covington 5, Zanesport 4.

They sat in the dressing room listening to the last inning between the Lakers and the Youngstown Boilermakers on the radio. The Lakers won it, and the Tanagers had dropped a full game out of the lead. The Lansing Senators, crowding second place hard, were due in tomorrow night. Mike Gaffney said to Furber, "Be ready tomorrow, Rube. You've got to be the stopper."

The Tanagers dressed in significant silence. Johnny

Gramner thought, A walk, a pop-out, a double and single. Not bad for the night. "What's Babe Tozer's batting average?" he asked of no one in particular.

Gaffney's eyes fired beanballs at his second sacker. "Never mind the individual averages, Gramner. You're on a team, or didn't I tell you?"

Johnny turned away. Sure, he knew, but a whole team isn't sold to the major leagues.

Gaffney said to Sam Berman, "Whitlow is off the active list. I'm bringing up a third baseman from Beloit."

"Can he heet?" Chico Gonzales asked.

"Right now his average is three sixty-seven," the manager said. "Name's Jorgeson."

Johnny tightened his lips. Just as Al Sava said, a guy could come up and they'd like his face better than yours. The first thing you knew you'd be shipped out like a case of prunes. As he left the dressing room it occurred to him that a player named Jorgeson was not on his mind, but a girl with soft brown eyes. There was a hunger in him that a big steak would never cure, a feeling he dared not analyze.

CHAPTER 11

T HE JINX FOLLOWED WILLIE FURBER TO THE MOUND when he faced the Lansing Senators. He couldn't find the plate with the letup pitch when he needed it, and his fast one wouldn't stay alive. The visitors beat him,

120

6–3. Johnny Gramner knocked in two of the runs and scored another. Mike Gaffney wired Robek and asked him to return as soon as he thought it possible. In the Tanager dressing room after the game, Furber picked up a Zanesport paper, scanned the sports page for a moment, then called to Johnny. "What do you know? The Carlton Braves won the pennant."

"Good for Dan Kelso," Johnny said. "I'll send him congratulations." He wondered if Al Sava had bet on the Laraine Robins when he'd left the Braves, and how much.

"The Portsmouth team did all right after I left," Furber said. "They finished well up. Goes to show nobody is indispensable, huh?"

Johnny ignored the rib. Mike Gaffney answered the pitcher. "No truer word was ever spoken, Rube. But I wish Arnie Hagen were with us."

Johnny Gramner glanced toward the manager, his mouth partly open. He did not get it. Arnie Hagen, a lame kid who took care of the batrack. Back on West Lancey, there had been very little of that stuff called morale, that intangible but vitally necessary lift a group of men rely on to reach a certain goal. The Tanagers had a lot of faith in Arnie Hagen, but Johnny Gramner was too much of an individualist to have discovered the sort of tonic the little bat boy gave the rest of the group.

"What do they pay that bat boy?" Johnny asked Stan Coveskie when they reached their hotel room. "Do they have to go by the scale set up by the magicians' union?"

"Hard as nails, aren't you?" the pitcher threw back at the second baseman. "I wish you—" He broke off and shrugged. "Oh, you wouldn't understand what I'm talking about. Well, maybe we win tomorrow, Johnny."

"Yeah, sure," the ballplayer said. "We've got to some-time."

The next night, under a sky heavy with the threat of rain, the Tanagers were trailing, 4–2, when Arnie Hagen came into the dugout. He had his uniform on; his face was thin and colorless. The home club was in for the last of the sixth, and Mike Gaffney said before going to the coach's box, "Arnie, what are you doin' out of bed? You look like the last run of shad. Better run home before you—"

"We're in a bad slump, Mr. Gaffney," the lame boy said. "Somebody has t' get you out." He picked up the loaded bat Sam Berman tossed aside before the fielder went up to lead off.

Johnny Gramner said, "Does he have to worry that much about his job? So Berman will belt one because the mascot came back. Ha!"

Sam Berman hit the second pitch and the ball hit the scoreboard in deep right. "What was that you were sayin', Gramner?" Nick Stenji asked as Leo Kleiner stepped in to hit.

The cleanup hitter took a strike, fouled off the Lansing southpaw's next two pitches, then lifted one high over the left-field barrier. Johnny Gramner, hitless so far that night, worked the string out, then singled through the hole between first and second. The Senators' manager came to the mound, conferred with his backstop, then signaled to his bull pen. The crowd began to sense that the Tanagers were out of their slump.

Pat O'Dowd drew a walk from the relief pitcher, and Nick Stenji bunted down the third-base line and advanced both runners. With one out, Mike Gaffney called Wally Felsch back from the plate and sent in the new kid,

122

Jorgeson, who had arrived at the park only an hour before. He was a rangy player with a nice pair of shoulders and Johnny watched him narrowly.

Jorgeson hit a long foul ball, then struck out with his bat on his shoulder. Johnny glanced at Mike Gaffney, but the manager showed no signs of impatience with the new man. Arnie didn't touch Jorgeson's bat with the rabbit's foot, Johnny thought.

Gaffney went to the bench again, had Rubeski hit for Coveskie. Rubeski obliged the home crowd by dropping a handle hit behind second. Johnny and O'Dowd were running with the pitch with two out, and both scored. Rubeski took second when the Lansing fielder threw too late to his catcher to try and nip O'Dowd. The Tanagers were in front, 5–4.

Preacher Marcum, sore back and all, went out to pitch for the Tanagers after Armitage popped to the infield. He held the Senators off the rest of the way, and a Kleiner homer with Jorgeson on base salted the game down for the home team.

In the dressing room Charley Agnew immediately took hold of Arnie. The bat boy's cheeks were flushed and there was an unhealthy shine in his eyes. "You crazy kid!" Agnew shouted. "You're running a fever." He yelled at the players, "We've got to get him in a cab and home fast."

"Well, we won." The bat boy grinned, and suddenly began to shiver.

"I'll take care of him," Mike Gaffney said. "Hurry up and get your uniform off, Arnie."

Stan Coveskie sidled up to Johnny Gramner. "I don't care what you call it," the pitcher said, "but I think that kid would rather die than see us blow this pennant."

Luck stayed with the Zanesport club. The rains came and lasted two days and gave Gaffney's pitchers a rest. Ted Robek arrived from Nebraska, and Arnie Hagen had the virus licked by the time the Topeka Redskins came in for a three-game series. A letter from Al Sava told Johnny Gramner that the man had dropped a bundle on the Laraine Robins. Johnny would have to boot the Zanesport team in to make up for the wallop to his bank roll, Sava wrote. After reading the letter, Johnny remembered that he hadn't sent Dan Kelso congratulations. Well, it was a little too late now. All his thoughts during the last two weeks of the pennant race would have to be on his hitting. His average now was .296. It had to go over .300. His contract for next year would be made out accordingly.

The pennant race went right down to the wire and when the Lake City Oilers came into Zanesport they were only one game behind. The three-game series would decide. Mike Gaffney was depending on Preacher Marcum and Willie Furber to bring the Tanagers the first flag in over eight years. During the last two weeks the writers had said that the difference had been Johnny Gramner. He had plugged up the hole at second base and he was hitting .301. His next stop, according to the experts, would be with Philadelphia, the parent club.

In the dressing room before the Saturday afternoon game, Speck Armitage stepped up to Johnny. "I got a couple of tickets for Dora for today's game, Johnny. I imagine she'll bring Madge."

"My luck to make an error or strike out," Johnny said. "I think she'd like that, Speck."

"We'll find out tonight, Johnny. We've got a date." The shortstop grinned.

124

Johnny whirled around, ready to protest, but Speck was going through the door to the runway. He picked up his glove and followed. The day had suddenly become brighter. The stands were jammed when the Tanagers took infield practice. Temporary bleachers had been set up in deep left. Across the way, Hobe Kilmer was beginning to warm up for the Lakers. The Tanagers had beaten him only twice in two years.

On the bench after practice, Speck said, "The gals are behind third base, Johnny. Give 'em a high sign when you take the field."

"If I go suddenly crazy," the second baseman said, "the writers will have me married to the girl before Monday morning."

"You should be that lucky," Speck said.

Speck, in Whitlow's absence, took the batting order out to the umpires. It was Armitage, Jorgeson, Robek, Kleiner, Gramner, O'Dowd, Stenji, Felsch, and Marcum.

Zanesport fans cut loose with a terrific roar when the Tanagers took the field. Johnny Gramner, off second, glanced toward the seats behind third and remembered a little blue and white hat. He stooped to pick up an imaginary pebble and tossed it away, banged his right fist into the palm of his glove, and called out, "Get 'em, Preacher."

Marcum looked at Johnny, brows lifted. The kid had never been a holler guy. He grinned when he turned to throw to the Lake City lead-off man. Maybe the kid was human. The Preacher proceeded to retire the side, and for the next five innings neither team got a runner to third. The Oilers began the sixth with their third hit off Marcum. The next man took a strike, two balls, and belted a foul over the right-field scoreboard, missing a

125

homer by only a few feet. The Preacher, careful, walked him and then faced Babe Tozer, the leading hitter of the league. Tozer also worked the Preacher for a walk, and Gaffney waved for the bull pen to show some life.

Dib Vallo, a .296 hitter for the Oilers, hit Marcum's first pitch and sent a lazy looper over second. There seemed to be no chance for the Tanager outfielders. The base runners were on the move as Johnny ran backward, then turned and raced toward the outfield. He made a dive and caught the ball inches from the ground, got to his feet, and fired to Jorgeson at third. Jorgeson fired to Armitage, covering second for the triple play, and a tremendous hand for the Tanager second baseman lasted for fully two minutes. Marcum waited for him to stroll in. "Thanks, Johnny," he said. "After that one we can't lose."

Johnny, embarrassed, grinned and looked toward third base. One of the girls waved to him, but she wasn't wearing a blue and white hat.

As Johnny stepped up to bat the Zanesport fans again roared their approval. After working the count to two and two, Johnny singled sharply to center field. Pat O'Dowd skied deep to the Oiler left fielder after fouling off two bunt attempts, and Nick Stenji struck out. Gaffney called Felsch back and brought Rubeski off the bench. The Tanager pinch hitter doubled to right and Johnny trotted home with the cheers ringing in his ears. As he rounded third, Gaffney clapped his hands and called out, "Nice goin', Johnny!"

Preacher Marcum gave up only one more hit the rest of the way. Now the Tanagers needed one more win to take the pennant.

A tall man with gray hair came into the Zanesport

dressing room and shook hands with Mike Gaffney, then looked toward Johnny Gramner. "Quite a boy, Mike. Maybe some day I'll have to take him away from you."

"It'll cost you," Mike said.

"So I've heard," the visitor said. Gaffney called Johnny over. "This is Terry Patten," Gaffney said. "He's a scout for the Philly Quakers."

Johnny's eyes widened as he shook hands with the important baseball man.

"You played a great game, Johnny," Terry Patten said. "I hope to see you up in the big leagues in a year or two."

A year or two! Johnny's smile vanished. This was a scout? What did he expect, blood? He said, "Glad to've met you," and walked away.

Patten turned to Gaffney. "A natural ballplayer, Mike, but how about his disposition?"

"You have to buy that, too." Gaffney grinned.

Johnny walked to the apartment house with Speck, and Dora met them at the door. She kissed Speck and laughed. "Why couldn't it have been you to start that triple play, busher? We could tell our kids about it."

Madge Wessler came forward slowly when Johnny walked into the living room, but she gave him a smile. "It was a beautiful catch," she said. "You could have just about everything in this town."

"Want t' bet?" Speck asked. Madge's face reddened and her eyes spiked Speck through and through. Johnny sat down, all doubt that he was in love with this girl gone from his mind. He was just as certain that she was as far away as the moon was from West Lancey Street. He was the pig's ear, he thought bitterly. She was the sleek velvet purse.

Speck Armitage took his girl by the arm. "We've got our own plans, Johnny. Why don't you teach the flash to play Scrabble, Madge?"

"Now wait," the second baseman choked out, suddenly thrown out far off the sack. "I—"

Madge said, "I'm tired, Johnny. I've put in fourteen straight hours at the hospital. You don't mind if we don't go out?"

"It's O.K.," Johnny said, and the girl sat down at the other end of the couch and observed him. "You're a strange guy," she said. "After you made that catch and the crowd went crazy applauding you, you didn't even tip your cap."

"Did you ever hear them boo me?" Johnny retorted. "Ted Williams lets the fans know what he thinks of them, and he doesn't bow and scrape to the crowd when he hits a homer."

"You're not Ted Williams. You're a rookie trying to get to the majors," Madge pointed out. "Did you read what one sportswriter said about you? That you're a businessman and that maybe the Tanagers should put a desk and chair at second base."

"Sportswriters!" Johnny said with disdain.

"They can make or break you," the girl said. "So can the fans. No ballplayer is bigger than the game, Johnny. You've got the worst inferiority complex I've ever seen. Off the diamond, I mean. Isn't there anyone you actually like?"

Madge threw this one fast and straight and he took his cut. "Yeah, there is. Who could help liking you?"

She dropped her eyes, a faint flush on her cheeks. "I'm glad, Johnny," she said. She got up and went to a desk in the corner of the room. "Do you play Canasta?"

128

"No," the ballplayer said ruefully. "I only know one game. I guess I'm a washout unless I've got a baseball suit on."

"You're never too old to learn." Madge began setting up the bridge table. It did not occur to Johnny that he should help her. The women did the work where he came from. The girl suddenly said, "Make yourself useful, Johnny. There are two folding chairs in the closet."

Two hours later Johnny Gramner left, full of waffles and maple sirup and a feeling that wasn't easy to analyze. All the way back to the hotel he called himself a sap. But she was different, he kept thinking. She didn't spread on the make-up, she offered no silly chatter, and she was smart. And most of all, she wasn't out to make a guy spend his money.

The Zanesport park was jammed to capacity again the next afternoon. The Oilers had to win both remaining games to tie for the pennant, and they had a left-hander, Early Wiltse, warming up. Mike Gaffney slapped Rube Furber on the back when the Tanagers filled their dugout and told him the flag was in his hands.

"I'll win it or throw my arm off." Willie grinned and went out to loosen up with the bull-pen catcher, Ray Mosser.

Johnny Gramner, coming in after infield practice, looked toward the seats behind third base. Madge Wessler was not there, and he had to admit he was disappointed.

Fighting for their lives, the Oilers made it an airtight ball game for seven innings and led, 1–0, when the Tanagers came to bat. Wiltse had been tough; his curve was finding the corners and his letup pitches had the heavy Zanesport hitters off balance. Ted Robek led off for the Tanagers, and Gaffney crossed up the opposition by ordering the slugger to lay one down. Robek dragged the bunt along the third-base line and beat it out for a hit. The crowd started pleading for a rally. Leo Kleiner, with thirty-seven homers for the campaign, hit a three-and-one pitch deep to left that the Oiler outfielder pulled in after a long run. Robek tagged up and then went to second, his slide just beating the throw-in.

The fans roared with anticipation when Johnny Gramner stepped into the batter's box. He'd been up twice, had walked and had sacrificed. He swung at Wiltse's first pitch, rifled it through the hole between first and second, and Robek came in with the tying run. Allie Renner, coaching at first, stepped up to the bag and cautioned him that picking the opposition off the initial sack was the Oiler pitcher's specialty.

"O.K.," Johnny said, and took his lead when Wiltse looked in at his catcher for the sign. Johnny took two more steps toward second, and then Wiltse fired to his first baseman. Johnny realized he was out before he hit the dirt. As he walked to the bench the crowd got on him. They'd already forgotten the run he'd driven in.

Pat O'Dowd doubled to right a few seconds later and Johnny knew he could have scored from first if he hadn't been picked off. Stenji was an easy out and the Tanagers took the field. Willie Furber got the first two men to face him, one on strikes, the other on a pop to Robek at first. And then the trouble started. The Oiler shortstop hit a Baltimore chop, the ball hitting home plate and bouncing high to the infield. The batter was on first before a throw could be made. Babe Tozer stepped in, and after Willie Furber had two strikes on him, he smashed a grounder a few feet to Johnny Gramner's right. It looked like a routine play, and the Tanager outfielders started

130

trotting in. The ball suddenly skipped over Johnny's glove and went out into shallow right. The base runner, on the move with two out, slid safely into third.

Johnny kicked dirt up. Willie Furber looked out at him and grinned. "Still two out," he said. "I'll get this one."

The batter swung at Willie's slider, let two bad ones go by, then hit a dribbler between the mound and the third-base line. Furber had to make the play. He fired to Ted Robek, but the runner beat the throw, and a run scored for Lake City.

Willie Furber struck the next man out and walked into the dugout shaking his head. Johnny Gramner followed him, his head down, knowing that his error could assume mammoth proportions. It could mean the pennant. Fans would never forget that.

Mike Gaffney used two pinch hitters but failed to even the score, and his heavy hitters were stopped by Wiltse in the ninth. The Tanagers went to the dressing room, still only one game ahead.

"So don't let it get you down, Johnny," Mike said in the dressing room. "The best of 'em make errors."

The second baseman sat on the bench, staring at the floor. The Oilers could even it on Tuesday night, and maybe win the play-off series. The writers, the fans, would go back to the error that had led to the visitors' win in the second game of the series. He thought of a pitcher named Branca who'd thrown the gopher ball that had put the New York Titans in a world series. Up to now he hadn't exactly lived it down. The fact that most of the players around him were shrugging the defeat off kindled Johnny's temper. What did they have to lose? They weren't aiming for the big leagues.

In the room at the Fairmount, Stan Coveskie grew weary of Johnny's gloomy post-mortems. The pitcher said, "If Speck or Jorgeson had booted it, would you still be griping? Because the Tanagers lost?"

"Meaning what?" Johnny Gramner asked.

"It seems personal to me," Stan said dryly.

"So if it is?" the second baseman snapped. "Who looks after Johnny Gramner if he gets skulled by a pitch, or any other way the skids are put under him?"

"Let's drop it," Coveskie said.

The door opened and Speck Armitage came in. He grinned at Johnny. "Dora sent you a message from Madge. She wants to know if you're going to let her get even on that canasta game."

"Yeah?" Johnny eyed Speck dourly. "That's where you're wrong. She's way ahead of me."

"That I know," the shortstop said. "But she's one in a million, the kind that's willing to wait until you catch up to her."

"It'll be a long time," Johnny said, smiling only with his mouth.

CHAPTER 12

T HE THIRD GAME OF THE CRUCIAL SERIES BETWEEN the Tanagers and the Oilers was a real Donnybrook. Stan Coveskie was knocked out in the third and Zanes-port came in trailing, 4–0. Gaffney's hitters began to tee off on the Oilers' Jocko Conley. Jorgeson singled to right, and Robek rattled a triple off the fence in deep center. Leo Kleiner, with only two hits in the series, doubled to right, and the manager of the Oilers strolled to the mound. A left-hander, Nino Pasquale, took over and Johnny Gramner promptly greeted him with a single through the middle. Kleiner came in with the third Tanager run.

Pat O'Dowd looked at a third strike, but Nick Stenji, catching the fever, pounded a double near the left-field foul line far out, and Johnny Gramner, running like a frightened deer, came all the way around to tie up the ball game. Rubeski, playing for Felsch, dropped a bunt in front of the plate; the Lake City catcher, too anxious, fired into the dirt at third, and Stenji was safe. Gaffney sent Sam Berman in to hit for DelGardo, the pitcher who had replaced Coveskie. The veteran skied deep to left and Stenji scored from third with the Tanager's fifth run of the inning. Speck Armitage hit at a three-and-one pitch and was out, short to first.

Preacher Marcum went in to pitch for the Tanagers and set the Oilers down until the sixth, when a Babe Tozer homer over the scoreboard with a man on put the visitors in front once more. The next man singled and then Marcum walked two men. The bases were loaded with only one out, and Gaffney went to the bull pen again. He gambled on Willie Furber.

The hitter worked him to a full count, with O'Dowd hotly protesting the last pitch. He kicked up dirt, banged his glove down, and got the heave-ho from the plate umpire. Ray Mosser went in to catch. The batter hit the next one far to Armitage's right, but he raced over, caught it, and scooped it to Gramner. Johnny leaped

133

and fired to first, and Robek dug it out of the dirt for the twin killing.

It was all Johnny Gramner after that. In the seventh he dived to his right, took a line drive from Tozer's bat three inches from the ground, and threw to Robek from a sitting position to double up the man who had headed for second. It was Johnny Gramner who doubled with the bases loaded in the eighth to put the Tanagers in front, 8–6, and it was his backhand stop close to the second sack with two Oilers on base that broke the back of a rally on the part of the visitors. He stepped on second and rifled to Robek for the third double play of the ball game. Willie Furber, the pressure off, struck out the next Lake City hitter, and Zanesport was the pennant winner.

The Tanagers chattered crazily in the dressing room and roughed Johnny around. He took it as gracefully as he knew how, thinking, They'll pay me next year. They're admitting I'm the difference.

But was he? A nagging voice within Johnny asked the question. Willie Furber, the rookie from the farm, had pitched some of the best games the league had seen in years. The double plays would have been impossible without Robek and Armitage. The Tanagers were a team, the voice kept saying, and without team play Johnny was just another good infielder who wielded a mighty bat. The sounds around him broke Johnny's reverie, brought him back to reality.

"Guess you'll go back to the home town and get the mayor to declare a holiday, Johnny," Mike Gaffney said. "What do you figure to do this winter?"

"Work," the ballplayer said. "Where I can keep in

134

shape. Bridge City?" Johnny laughed. "I said if I ever got away from it, I'd never go back."

The writers were there full force. One mentioned the reason the Philly Quakers were losing the pennant in the National League—a weak-hitting infield with the exception of Wessler on first. He said, "You won't have Gramner very long, Gaffney."

"We'll cross that bridge when we get to it." The manager laughed and walked over to Johnny. "I've got a couple of garages here in town," he said to his keystone man. "If you want to work for me—nothing that will risk ruining your hands, understand? Washing cars, gassing them up, all that, Johnny."

"Thanks, but I don't think so." Johnny shook his head. A guy like Gaffney would do you a favor, but the day would come when he would throw it at you. He'd find his own job. Chico Gonzales was going back to Mexico to play some winter ball, and he'd asked Johnny to come along. "No thanks, Chico," he had told him. "I will not risk breaking a leg on those crumby fields."

Johnny wanted to stay in Zanesport but would not admit the real reason. A week after the season had closed he got a job as checker in a lumberyard and found a cheap room on the south side of town. During the weeks that followed, Madge was on night duty and he saw her only twice. And then on Christmas Eve he bought her a compact and walked across town to give it to her.

Madge answered the door. Speck's girl, Dora, had gone to Pennsylvania for the holidays. When Johnny walked into the apartment he saw a man a little older than himself sitting on the sofa. The man got up and smiled. "Don't tell me, Madge. Who doesn't know Johnny Gramner in Zanesport?"

"This is Paul Norton, Johnny. An intern at the hospital. Won't you sit down?"

"Glad to meet you," Johnny said.

He saw the big package, beautifully wrapped, on the coffee table, and knew this guy had brought it for Madge. It occurred to him with a shock that a man can have competition off the diamond, too. The doctor was good-looking, Johnny admitted, and he had all the social graces.

"Won't you have a cup of coffee with us, Johnny?" Madge asked.

"I'm sorry," he said. "I just thought I'd stop by and— wish you Merry Christmas. I have to run along."

"Thank you, Johnny." Madge sat down next to the intern. "The same to you. Aren't you going home?"

"No," he said and walked toward the door, forgetting the small package in his pocket. "Glad to meet you, Doc. See you, Madge."

There were sharp teeth in the wind that blew in his face as he walked toward his rooming house. The cold was as bitter as his thoughts. At the corner he took the Christmas package from his pocket and threw it into a trash can. O.K., he thought, her league is not for me.

At his rooming house, he found a letter from Speck Armitage on the hall table. Speck had a good deal up in the Laurentians. A ski lodge. Back in his room he read the letter. Speck asked him how he and Madge were getting along. "*. . . don't forget, Johnny,*" the shortstop had written, "*you can't expect to have a good batting average if you don't stay in the line-up. You're not the only single guy in town. Madge doesn't have to sit on the bench and wait, pal. You've made a lot of hits, but have you made one with her? Business is booming up* *here. I heard that Robek's mother died. If you see. . . ."*

Johnny crumpled the letter into a ball and rifled it to the wastebasket, knowing that Speck had written the truth. He had been afraid to see too much of the girl, knowing that he would have to tell her how he felt and that he was afraid of what her reaction would be. Besides, responsibilities could ruin the goal he had sworn to reach. He felt mixed up. Suddenly he decided to go home. He could be in Bridge City by ten in the morning if snow did not fall and block the roads. He hurriedly packed a bag; twenty minutes later he was on the bus out of Zanesport.

West Lancey looked no happier to Johnny Gramner in Christmas dress than it had on any other day. As he walked up the flights of stairs to his mother's flat, the familiar sounds and the smells were no sweeter than before. He paused outside the door, hearing his mother's strident voice railing at his brother. "Merry Christmas," he mumbled without feeling and swung the door open.

His mother stared at him for a moment, a brightness slowly coming to her tired eyes. Ricky dropped a comic magazine to the floor and said, "Well, it's the big man! The Zanesport flash! Dig those clothes. Hi, Johnny, what made you come home?"

"Santa Claus," Johnny said and gave his mother an embarrassed kiss on the cheek. A small tree stood in a corner of the room, sparsely decorated, and a few packages were piled at its base. A paper wreath hung at each window.

There was a brashness in Ricky that angered Johnny until he realized how he had battled his way on this street. The kid was wearing flashy clothes, and he sported

137

a wrist watch. "Kind of sharp." Johnny grinned at his brother. "Still working for Al Sava?"

"Yeah," Ricky said. "Who else?"

"He's gettin' too big for his britches, Johnny," Mrs. Gramner said. "He's in a gang callin' themselves The Black Tigers. He's out all hours, and when I ask him where he's been and what he's doin' he says it's none of my business."

"It ain't," Ricky said. "I earn my own money, so I do as I please."

"I'll take a hand to you in a minute," his mother snapped. "You're not so tough yet I can't—"

Johnny Gramner said, his nerves strumming, "Look, both of you are forgetting it's Christmas." He thought of the orderly lives of the people in his new world and was not too glad he'd come back, even for a little while. "What do you do for Al, Rick?"

"All sorts of things," Ricky said. "He pays me good because my brother is a hot ballplayer. He claims you owe it to him."

"Yeah? Maybe I do." He got up and reached for his coat. "It's only right I drop in and see Al for a few minutes, Ma. I won't be long."

Al Sava lived in a second-rate hotel two blocks away, and when Johnny knocked on his door, a hard-bitten looking man opened it a few inches and peered out at him. "Who wants to see Al?"

"Johnny Gramner."

The tough's eyes widened and then Al roared, "Johnny Gramner? Let him in, you knucklehead."

Al looked a little fatter, and there was something different about his eyes. They seemed troubled, Johnny thought. "Yeah, this is my boy!" he said loudly and

138

slapped the ballplayer on the back. "I made him, Buster."

Johnny sat and listened to the old story about the discarded big league ballplayer. "You got 'em where you want 'em now, Johnny," Sava said. "They want ivory they need, you tell 'em how much it'll cost 'em. I've steered you right so far, haven't I? Don't give any of the suckers an even break. It's a business, and I bet you've found it out."

Johnny Gramner, although not aware of it at the moment, had returned to Bridge City to make some repairs to his armor. Men like Mose Watson, Dan Kelso, Speck Armitage, had been making dents in it. A girl with brown eyes had cracked it wide. "You're right, Al," he said. "It's every man for himself." The words sounded hollow to him.

Later, having Christmas dinner with his mother and Ricky, he decided to leave town that night. He explained that he had to be on the job early on Monday morning and would need some rest.

"A hot-shot, Ma," Ricky said. "Too big for us. Look, he even wears a tie."

"What's this Black Tiger deal?" Johnny asked.

"Protection." The boy grinned. "You should know."

Johnny did know. His anger cooled when he remembered what he'd been at the same age. You had to be tough to survive on this street. Well, let him find his way out, he told himself. He gave his mother a twenty-dollar bill and told her to buy a new dress, and for the first time in many years, saw her cry. "I'm afraid," she told him. "I don't know why. I wish you were staying here."

"Try and give your mother a break," he said to Ricky. "Don't get in trouble."

"Get him!" Ricky smirked, and snatched a comic book

139

from the table. "Send me a baseball bat when you play with the Yanks."

He pictured Madge here seeing and hearing all this, and knew it could never happen. On the way to the bus terminal an hour later he guessed the intern would have the field to himself. Johnny Gramner had places to go. He had to stay tough to reach them. On the bus he recalled what Al had said when he left: "Remember, Johnny, I dropped a wad of cash on the Laraine Robins. On your say-so that the Braves couldn't make it with you leavin' the team. So if you get into any big dough, I figure you might send me some of it."

He tried not to think of another bus ride out of Carlton, but he could still hear the sound of a girl's voice above the monotonous singing of the heavy tires, and was glad when someone turned on a radio. Some of the passengers around him started singing along with the music. Halfway to Zanesport the snow started falling, and Johnny thought, It will soon be New Year's and then February and March. The Tanagers will loosen up around April. Forget West Lancey and Madge. Think of the contract that will come through the mail before very long. He should have asked Al how a guy holds out for part of the purchase price when a big league team makes a deal.

As the bus rolled across the flat highways to Zanesport, Johnny's thoughts unwillingly returned to West Lancey Street. Something about the scene jarred him, though he didn't know what it was. If only his mother and Rick could get away from there. Johnny could get them away from the drab flat, he knew, if he hit the big time next year, got a healthy cut of the purchase price.

But what was he thinking about? Nobody had gotten him away from West Lancey, he'd had to do it himself.

140

He'd had to fight all the way. Rick could do the same if he had any push. Besides, what could you do for a kid like that? As for his mother—maybe she'd done the best she could after his father died. Someday, he thought, he could give her something better than twenty dollars for a dress, something that would take the frightened look out of her eyes.

The contract reached Johnny in January. It called for a thousand more than the previous campaign, and he returned it with a letter asking for another five hundred and suggesting a clause be added in the event of a major league deal. The Zanesport front office asked him to come in and talk it over, and when Johnny appeared, Mike Gaffney was sitting in. The manager eyed his second baseman narrowly and advised him to keep his two feet on the ground. "You're not that big, Johnny. Not that important."

The ballplayer grinned. "The newspapers tell the story, Mr. Gaffney. I hit three hundred two in this league, and my fielding average was higher than any other second baseman in the league. If you don't think I'm worth what I ask, send me to some other ball club. The Omaha Packers could use an infielder."

The general manager of the Zanesport club argued with Johnny. He told him that Ted Robek and Leo Kleiner had signed their contracts and that they had contributed a lot to the success of the Tanagers.

"I'm not interested in what other people do," the ballplayer said. "I'm thinking of Johnny Gramner. Robek and Kleiner are old men in baseball and are going nowhere."

They finally settled on a bonus clause and inserted two or three lines in the contract that would take care of

Johnny if a major league club wanted to buy him. The Zanesport morning paper carried the story. The writers intimated that he struck a bargain as hard as he did a triple or a double. The inference that the Tanager infielder had a high regard for his own ability was made very plain, and reporters recalled his indifference to the accolade of the Zanesport fans. Who cared about criticism, however, when a man was on his way to the bank?

A week after he'd signed, Johnny got the scare of his young life. A plank fell off a truck in the lumberyard and the end of it hit Johnny on the wrist. He ground his teeth with pain and hurried to the office for first aid. He sat in a chair afterward, more scared than hurt, beads of perspiration around his mouth. "Tell the boss I'm going to the hospital," he told the girl in the office. "I want to make sure it isn't broken."

At Union hospital the X rays showed no more than a bad bone bruise. After more treatment Johnny left, a great load off his mind. As he passed the information desk downstairs he saw Madge Wessler coming along the corridor with Paul Norton. He stopped and waited for them. The girl gave him the smile that always stirred him, and the intern said, "Hi, Johnny. What brings you here?"

"Got hit at the lumberyard," he explained. "Can't take chances, Doc."

"I read the papers, Johnny," Madge said. "I see what you mean. You are a valuable asset to the Zanesport ball club."

"I have to take care of myself," Johnny said a little impatiently. "A ballplayer's only got seven to ten years."

"And after that, Johnny?" the girl asked. "You'll live like a hermit with your newspaper clippings? Have you forgotten you're always welcome at our place?"

142

"I'll stop in when I get a chance," Johnny said. "Maybe the doc can check on this wrist."

Madge Wessler flushed, but a little smile played around her lips. "He'll send you a bill, Johnny. He has to take care of himself, too."

And maybe you too, Johnny thought, as he left the hospital. It was beginning to dawn on him that baseball was not going to be quite enough to sustain him in future years.

Johnny Gramner stopped in at the girls' apartment the night before he left for Biloxi, the Tanagers' training camp. Speck Armitage was there and he ran to Johnny and shook his hand. "We're celebrating tonight, Flash. Show him the rock, Dora."

Dora stretched out her left hand and Johnny saw the diamond ring on the engagement finger. He grinned roguishly at Speck. "Another good guy hooked. You'd better hit better this year, Speck. You've got more to support than some of Gaffney's pitchers."

"Always the businessman." The shortstop laughed. "You're the guy I feel sorry for."

"Where's the M.D.?" Johnny asked.

"Paul?" Madge picked up a tray of canapés from the coffee table. She made a little face. "A new nurse came to the hospital a week ago. A redhead. Paul hasn't been the same since."

Johnny suddenly said, wondering if it was really he speaking, "Well, what are we waiting for, Speck? Let's get on with the celebration."

It was late when the two players left the girls. Madge said to Johnny, "The best of luck, and please remember what I told you a while ago. The fans like a star ballplayer to be more than a machine. They want him to be a human being like themselves. They like to believe you're making those hits and fancy plays for them as well as yourself. You could be a real nice fellow, Johnny. Keep trying."

CHAPTER 13

AT THE TRAINING CAMP, JOHNNY LEARNED THAT Wally Felsch and utility infielder Narin, along with pitchers Hardeman and Lundell, had been traded only a few days ago. Four rookies and a relief pitcher from the Pittsburgh Corsairs of the National League had put up at the hotel. A kid fresh from a college campus was due in any day, Gaffney told the writers. He'd pitched two no-hitters for Garfield University the previous year.

The first day of spring training was confined to loosening up the arms by throwing the ball, after a lap or two around the enclosure for every man on the squad. Gaffney warmed up a pitcher for the initial batting practice and sent the others out for a pepper game. He kept changing his practice pitchers, giving the staff a chance to rid their arms of winter kinks. At four thirty in the afternoon he ordered infield and outfield practice, and at five sent them all to the showers.

They were in the hotel lobby three days later when a gangly kid carrying a cheap suitcase came in and asked for Gaffney. The players were grouped near the news-

144

stand waiting for the bus to take them to the ball park. Johnny pointed the manager out to the visitor and grinned at Ted Robek. "Fresh from the milking stool," he said. "Wonder what he wants."

The kid's name was Andy Gardner. He told Mike he'd come down to try for the ball club at his own expense. He was a third baseman.

"Takin' the bread out of my mouth, huh?" Jorgeson said, grinning. "At cut prices yet."

The kid smiled, showing extra large teeth. His nose wrinkled. "I wouldn't do that, sir," he said, and his eyes were pleading as they shifted to Mike. "I got enough t' keep me for about three weeks. That ought t' be time enough to see if I—"

Gaffney said, "Got a glove and some baseball shoes?"

"I got the glove," Gardner said sheepishly. "I didn't know I had t' furnish the shoes."

Mike Gaffney looked at the hopeful rookie, then at Johnny Gramner, and wished the personalities could be switched. He said, "Get on the bus with us. We'll dig up a pair of shoes."

At the end of the week, Gaffney called the rookie over to the bench after a five-inning practice game. "Look, son," he said frankly, "don't waste any more of your money. You're two years away. You haven't hit a curve ball yet. Maybe some day you can make another try."

Tears were in Andy Gardner's eyes as he stood in front of Mike, his eyes fixed to the ground. "Thanks like everythin'—for lettin' me play this long." He looked up when Johnny Gramner strolled by. "I sure wish I was him, Mr. Gaffney. I'd play just for my keep an' railroad fare."

The second baseman came over and banged the

youngster on the back with a gloved hand. "Tough," he said. "But you either have it or you don't. Better luck next time."

In the dressing room later, a lot of the Tanagers were unusually silent. Leo Kleiner broke the tension. "I was rootin' for that kid, Mike. When you love the game like that you have a right to be born with the necessary talent for it."

"It's life," the manager said. "People take lots of things for granted. You don't appreciate a thing until you find out you can't have it."

Johnny Gramner looked up quickly. He knew the shoe fitted him. For the first time he realized something he had missed, the wholesome respect and admiration of the team of which he was a part.

He wanted that respect, and he wanted the crowds to like him as Johnny Gramner, not just as the big bat. But he didn't know how to get it. Sometimes he sensed that he'd said the wrong things, that his words sounded harsh and uncompromising. He'd felt sorry for young Gardner, but he couldn't show it, couldn't even admit it to himself. Because if he got soft and sentimental, he'd never get ahead. You got to the top in this game by stepping on the other guys. Sava had drummed that into him, and nothing about life in Bridge City had ever shown him any other way. Johnny felt a little disgusted with himself for the way his thoughts lately had been betraying what he knew to be his deepest convictions about life.

Pat O'Dowd was moving among the players making up a purse to give to Andy, and Mike Gaffney announced, "I want five bucks from every one of you."

After Andy had gone, Charley Agnew started patching up the casualties. Rubeski had a slide burn and the trainer applied soap and water, then five per cent

146

sulfathiazole. Steve Coveskie had a bad blister to be treated, and Mike Gaffney examined the spike wound on Pat O'Dowd's leg and advised the veteran catcher to get a booster tetanus shot. There were two Charley horses, and a slightly sprained ankle. The manager went over to the new outfielder, Steve McHenry, and grasped his left hand.

"A ring? You mean to say you were playing with that on?" Gaffney roared. "How long have you been in this game?"

"To tell the truth, Mr. Gaffney, I forgot," McHenry said.

"Don't forget again. And you, Browne, your nails are too long! You can have 'em torn off easy." Mike Gaffney picked up his windbreaker and started for the bus.

The Tanagers developed unusually well. At the end of three weeks, five rookies, having been found wanting, packed up and left the resort town. Curt Simonson, the college hurler, and Harvey Drew, the ex-big league fireman, got Gaffney's stamp of approval. After several intrasquad games, the Tanager pilot benched Nick Stenji in favor of a rookie, Pete Cuzco. Cuzco had been hitting well since his arrival. The batting order Gaffney would present against the opposition in the exhibition games was practically set: Armitage, Jorgeson, Robek, Kleiner, Gramner, O'Dowd, McHenry, Cuzco, and the pitcher.

Gramner had shown Gaffney that he was no flash in the pan. He was even surer around the keystone sack, and he was hitting the practice pitchers for a .318 average. The reporters, however, were hardly singing his praises, and one of them, in a particularly caustic column, referred to him as Johnny Grabner.

"The price of fame," Speck Armitage, sharing a room

with Johnny, said, and tossed the newspaper aside. "But you have to admit you strike a hard bargain."

"The club still comes out ahead," Johnny said. "They didn't have to keep me on this team, Speck. The Lakers would have grabbed me in a minute, and the front office knew it."

"Sure," Speck said. "But you're on record as a shrewd bargainer and that will be in the notebooks of every big league scout. You may be a player they have in mind, one of two they want to bring up. The other ballplayer could be pretty good himself, and he could be picked because of his record of meeting the club owners half-way. But you've got to maintain a steady batting average and keep getting most everything hit your way, or you'll find yourself behind the eight ball. What I'm trying to say is, a guy's temperament counts an awful lot, Johnny."

"Sure, I know," the second baseman said. "Probably everybody will be rooting for me to fall flat on my face because I held out for all that's coming to me."

"I know one person isn't thinking that way, Johnny," Speck said. "Madge. Have you written her?"

"She sent me a card," Johnny said. "I haven't had time to answer it. And what do I say to her anyway?"

" 'Having fine time, wish you were here,' " Speck grinned. "You're not that dumb, Johnny. You are in love with that girl, but you refuse to admit it. She doesn't exactly hate you, you know that."

"See if there's any good movies in town," the second baseman said.

A few days later, the Tanagers played the Shreveport club of the Gulf League, and Gaffney tried Curt Simonson on the mound. The ex-collegian fought his control for three innings and was saved by a great outfield catch by Steve McHenry and a double play started by Johnny Gramner. After three and a half innings, Shreveport led, 2–0, and then the Tanagers knocked the opposing pitcher out. Pete Cuzco opened the inning with a triple and scored on Rubeski's pinch sacrifice fly to left. Speck Armitage singled, and Jorgeson walked. Ted Robek stepped in and drove a ball almost to the gulf, and the Tanagers were in front by 4–2. Leo Kleiner and Johnny Gramner grounded to the infield.

Preacher Marcum came in to pitch and immediately got into trouble when two ground balls eluded the Zanesport infielders on the bumpy diamond. Johnny Gramner got the signal from Pat O'Dowd, and knew Marcum had it, too. The base runner off second was ducking back when Speck made a move toward second. And then Speck moved over nearer third, deep.

Marcum fooled with the rosin bag and got set to make his delivery. The Shreveport base runner took his lead, and then Marcum whirled and fired to the keystone sack. Johnny Gramner was there to take the throw and he nipped the runner by a foot.

The batter drove one deep to short and Speck dug it out, fired underhand to Johnny Gramner. Johnny pivoted and blazed it to Robek, and the Preacher was out of the inning. The Tanagers came in and nearly batted around. Johnny Gramner got hold of one with two on and two out and rattled the ball off the old fence in deep right; Zanesport led, 9–2. Pat O'Dowd ended the agony for the Shrevesport hurlers by fouling out to the catcher.

Gaffney rested Marcum and sent the ex-big leaguer, Harvey Drew, in. The visitors got one hit the rest of the way. A Mobile writer came into the Tanager dressing room later, a thin man with a lazy Southern drawl. He

149

shook hands with Mike Gaffney. "Came to get the low-down on your golden boy, Mike. Is it true the club's going to carry a cash register to ring up his extra-base hits?"

Johnny had good ears. He slammed his shirt down and walked over to the sports reporter. "You work on a second-rate sheet because you haven't got the brains to get on a big one. Maybe you make a hundred a week. Maybe you'd turn down an offer of one-fifty from Chicago or New York! Or would you feel sorry for your boss and stay in Mobile for peanuts? You get what you're worth, mister."

"No offense, Gramner," the writer said, backing away from the threat in the ballplayer's eyes. "Didn't you expect some ribbing after putting the pressure on a Class AA ball club after a few weeks in that league? It was baseball news, Gramner."

"Put this in your paper," Johnny snapped. "I'll keep demanding what I think I'm worth."

Gaffney got his second baseman by the arm and drew him away. "You've said enough for one day, Johnny. Cool off and get your shower."

Gaffney's voice cut through Johnny's fury. Why had he blown up that way? Why did he have to put some fresh reporter in his place? Get along with the boys from the papers, everyone had been telling him lately. They like you, they tell the public; the big leagues like a popular player, it'll help you get ahead.

That's what they said, but Johnny wasn't sure. They liked the hits, the grandstand plays, and the heck with the personality boys. He'd have plenty of time to butter reporters and win the popularity contests after he got to the top, the second baseman thought. But the little

150

voice within him said, "Will you? Will you get there this way? And if you get there, will you stay if the crowds get on you?"

The Tanagers won them all in the Cotton States League. They broke camp the second week in April and went to Atlanta to play the parent team, the Philly Quakers, in a three-game series. Two hours after Speck and Johnny had arrived at the hotel, the phone rang. The shortstop answered it and turned to Johnny. "A guy downstairs to see you. Mel Wessler, the—"

"Huh?" Johnny felt both excited and a trifle wary. "Tell him to come on up."

The first baseman for the Quakers stepped into the room a few minutes later and looked Johnny over carefully as he gave him his hand. Weeks of exposure to the Southern sun had darkened his lean face. His eyes were that soft brown color Johnny had cause to remember. Wessler said, "Wanted to meet you, Johnny. Madge mentions you a lot when she writes."

Speck shook hands with the big leaguer and then headed for the door. "I think I'll run down to the lobby and pick up some post cards, Johnny. Guess I'll see a lot of you tomorrow, Mel."

"Right," Wessler said and grinned wide.

"How is Madge?" Johnny asked, and pointed to the easy chair near the bed.

"Fine," the ballplayer said. "I think more of her than anybody else in this world, Johnny. I've heard quite a lot about you lately. You're a pretty good ballplayer, they tell me, but a tough character otherwise. I'll be frank, kid. Don't ever hurt Madge. Not in any way!"

"I don't know what you mean."

Mel Wessler's eyes did not lose their mildness. "I'm

151

sure you do, Johnny," he said. "If you haven't any idea of including Madge in your future plans, let her know as easy as you know how. Her letters convince me that she's a little overboard for you. Would you mind telling me how you feel about her?"

"Did she tell you to come here and look me over like I was a promising relief pitcher or something?" Johnny asked, his temper close to the surface again.

Wessler shook his head. "No. She asked me to drop in and see you and say 'hello.' The questions are on my own."

"Then I don't see that it's any of your business."

Wessler's eyes remained calm. "Look, Johnny, you've got to learn sooner or later that what you or I do affects the lives of others, both on and off the ball field. You can't lock yourself up in a world of your own, with a private moon and sun. I've looked out for Madge since I was seventeen. I've had to be a father to her." He got up from his chair. "All right, Johnny, I've paid my call. If you ever hurt her, expect some lumps of your own."

"I'm scared," Johnny said. "Maybe we'll give you hot-shots some lumps tomorrow."

"We can't wait, busher!" Wessler said and walked out.

Johnny stood staring at the closed door. Now what had he done? And what did the Quaker first baseman mean about hurting Madge? Madge was a swell girl, he liked her better than he wanted to admit, but after this showdown with her brother, Johnny figured, he'd never see her again. Yeah, somebody was going to get hurt, but it wasn't the girl with the brown eyes. The more he thought about it, the more angry he felt—angry at Mel Wessler for butting in, angry at Johnny Gramner for yapping back, angry at the whole dirty world in which he always had to fight everybody and everything to get ahead.

Speck came back a few minutes after the big leaguer had left and saw at once that Johnny was riled. He thought he knew why, but discreetly refrained from asking.

"If we never win another ball game, Speck," Johnny said, banging a fist against a pillow, "let's take the Quakers tomorrow."

"We could," Speck said. "They'll be using most of their second-string players, don't forget."

Beginning at two thirty the next afternoon, Johnny began living the worst baseball game of his young life. Bucky O'Doul, the Philly manager, looking ahead to a possible rebuilding of an aging infield, had doubtlessly instructed his players to give Gaffney's prize fielder the full treatment. The Quakers got on Johnny from the start, and when he stepped into the batter's box to face O'Doul's left-hander, Ferrill, the bench jockeys pulled out all stops.

"Hey, it's Gramner, Bucky. Lock up the safe!"

"So that's the wonder who is after my job, Frank! He stands up there like he's got ants."

"Hey, busher! Are you as good as you say?"

"Don't hit him, Wick, or we won't have no farm club!"

Boiling inside, Johnny slammed Ferrill's second pitch over short for a single, and when he took over first he said to Mel Wessler, holding the bag against him, "That his fastest pitch?"

The Quaker first sacker grinned. Johnny took his lead, chuckling over the hit against the big league hurler. And then he heard a warning cry from Sam Berman,

153

coaching at first. He tried to get back, but Wessler tagged him two feet off the bag. The first baseman said, "That's the first lesson, Johnny."

Ferrill struck out Pat O'Dowd and McHenry, and the minor league club took the field.

Stan Coveskie, pitching for the Tanagers, got Frohme, the Quaker right fielder, to sky to Leo Kleiner. Mel Wessler came up and smashed Coveskie's third pitch to right field, not too deep. Leo Kleiner charged the ball and came up with it. Wessler kept on going when he saw the Tanager fielder delay his throw-in. Johnny Gramner jumped to the bag and Kleiner fired the ball to him. Wessler slid in, saw that he was a little late, and kicked the ball out of Johnny's reach. He got up and dusted himself off, wearing a broad grin.

"Now, Mel," a falsetto voice came from the Quaker dugout. "That was not ver–r–r–y nice!"

Johnny went back to his position, his jaws set. A few moments later, the Quaker home-run hitter and cleanup man, Eddie Wyrosnik, drove one at him that seemed to have been fired from a gun. The ball hit against his stomach, knocking the wind out of him, and rolled to Robek at first. Wessler rounded third and scored, and Wyrosnik was at second ahead of Robek's throw to Armitage. Agnew came in to look Johnny over, and the Quakers sharpened their harpoons.

"Somebody get a peach basket! There should be some in Georgia."

"Drag him off. He's blockin' the base line."

There was no error on the play. The scoreboard recorded a hit for Wyrosnik, but Johnny Gramner felt no satisfaction over the decision. He told Agnew in a choking voice that he was all right, and went back to his position.

In the sixth, with the score 8–1 in favor of the big league club, Johnny Gramner came up to face O'Doul's second pitcher, Mogridge. Leo Kleiner was on third with a triple, and there was only one man down. Mogridge threw one in that burned close to Johnny's chin and he did a fancy step getting out of the way.

"Ah, Pavlova!" a Quaker bench jockey yelled.

Johnny took a cut at the next pitch and missed, going to one knee on the follow-through. He knew as he stepped in again that he had never seen such speed in the minor league. Mogridge looked him over, fired a change of pace that Johnny let go by. Two strikes. Mogridge tried to make him bite on two bad ones, but he kept his bat on his shoulder, trying not to hear the riding from the bench.

The next pitch was to his liking and he got the good wood on it and guessed this would put a gag on his tormentors. The ball screamed toward right field, but as he legged it to first he saw Mel Wessler leap high and get it in the webbing of his mitt. The small hinterland crowd cut loose with an amazed roar, and Johnny Gramner put on the brakes and walked toward the Tanager bench.

"That's the way we do it here, son," a Quaker on the bench said.

The game ended with the minor league club beaten by a 10–3 score. Johnny slumped on the bench in the dressing room, and Gaffney came over and patted him on the back.

"Didn't you get it through your head they were deliberately singling you out, Johnny?" the manager asked. "O'Doul wanted to see what stuff you had in you. Even

Eddie Collins would have been handcuffed by Wyrosnik's smash when he was in his prime. That last one you connected with would have been a hit ninety-nine times out of a hundred. You didn't look half as bad as you think you did. Tomorrow's another day, kid."

"That's a bunch of real ballplayers," Ted Robek said. "They know every angle, every little trick. That's the majors, my friends."

Still deflated, Johnny left the Atlanta ball park with Speck and Steven McHenry half an hour later. Goggle-eyed minor league fans were blocking the exit getting autographs from the big leaguers. Johnny felt the tightness of misgiving in his stomach. The chastening at the hands of experts was having its effect on him.

Speck said laughingly, "Well, they liked us in Zanesport."

CHAPTER 14

AFTER BREAKFAST, JOHNNY READ THE ATLANTA *Sun-Star's* sports page. The headlines said: "QUAKERS RIP FARM CLUB, 10–3. *Wyrosnik and Delennis Homer!*" The smaller print said that Zanesport's prize rookie, Gramner, looked uncertain in his first game against the big leaguers. The sun was shining, but a day never looked gloomier to Johnny Gramner. Speck Armitage was reading a letter he'd picked up at the desk, and a beatific grin wreathed his round face.

156

"They miss us, Johnny," the shortstop said. "Dora's been shopping for furniture, and has a line on an apartment. How lucky can a schmoe like me get?"

"They gave me an error when Wessler kicked the ball out of my glove," Johnny griped, and tossed the newspaper aside.

The shortstop said, "An autopsy on you would show a trademark of a baseball manufacturing firm on what you call a heart. Sure, we lost to the Quakers. Last year seven other big league teams lost a lot to the same ball club. We're not expected to beat those guys."

Johnny went out of the room and walked toward the elevators. When he got to the lobby, a husky sunburned man spoke his name. It was the Quaker's Wyrosnik. "Mornin', Gramner. We rode you pretty hard yesterday. But no more than we do the New York club. You're a pretty good looking ballplayer, kid. Sit down."

The Tanager second baseman had no sooner dropped into a chair when four other major leaguers made their appearance. One was the veteran keystone man for O'Doul. He asked Johnny about his family, and how he'd started to play the game, and began giving him some friendly advice about playing the middle sack. They ribbed him about the ball Wyrosnik had slammed into his meridian, and he was surprised to find himself enjoying it.

Then Bucky O'Doul came over, a big cigar jutting from his mouth, and Johnny wanted to get up and run for the elevators. O'Doul said, "Hello, Gramner. Did we scare you out there yesterday?" He grinned at Ferrill. "Be nice to him, Wick. Some day he'll be behind you maybe when you need a double play to get you out of a hole."

157

"I'll be around three years from now?" Ferrill said.

The attention restored Johnny Gramner's confidence, and he vowed to show these big timers some baseball when the arc lights were turned on at eight o'clock. But he knew that he wanted to do more than show them. He had sensed some of the camaraderie, the zest these players got from an afternoon on the diamond. Johnny wanted to share that, too.

This hotel was big, and the food was something he'd only read about back on West Lancey Street. Fresh white tablecloths and silver coffee pots, a waiter treating a guy like a visiting diplomat. It was strawberries and cream after a diet of stewed prunes, and some day, he promised himself, this would be more than a transitory luxury.

A sizable crowd came out to see the Quakers tear into their farm club again. Willie Furber, however, had his fast ball smoking and fully alive, and the big leaguers, at the end of the third inning, had garnered but one hit off the Tanager farmer boy. Johnny Gramner stepped into the batter's box to lead off the top of the fourth for Gaffney, and the Quakers sharpened their spurs and began to ride. O'Doul had veteran Sam Judson, a sixteen-game winner the previous season, pitching. Judson had whiffed the Tanager second sacker in the second inning on three pitched balls.

"One out, Sam!" a bench jockey yelled.

"Bend one around him! He'll cut at it!"

Johnny took a called strike, watched Judson's waste pitch go by. He cut hard at a curve ball and slammed it deep to left field for two bases, and the crowd, always for the underdog, gave him a tremendous hand. Judson

158

looked at Johnny and grinned as he rubbed up the ball. He tried his knuckler and lost control of it, and Gaffney waved Johnny to third. The second baseman slid in ahead of the catcher's frantic throw. A few moments later O'Dowd hit the three-and-one pitch high to center, and Johnny Gramner came in with the Tanager run. Judson struck out McHenry and induced Cuzco to ground out to Wessler.

Willie Furber, as the crowd watched breathlessly, got the Quakers out again on three fly balls. The pitcher led off in the fourth and dragged a bunt along the first-base line. The Quaker catcher picked it up ten feet from the plate, dropped it, then threw too late to get Willie. Speck Armitage stepped in and looked over at Mike Gaffney behind third. He took a ball, a strike, then laid one down along the third-base line. The Quaker third baseman ran in, stopped, hoping the trickler would roll foul. It went dead right on the white line, and two men were on for the farm club.

Jorgeson, horse-collared the day before, clubbed Judson's first pitch into the gap between the Quaker right and center fielders. The ball rolled to the fence and Furber and Armitage scored. Jorgeson pulled up at third, and O'Doul came out of the Philly dugout. He conferred with his catcher and half the Quaker ball club on the mound for a few moments, then signaled for a new pitcher.

Ted Robek faced the fireman, Shelby, and hit a three-and-one pitch high to the infield, but Leo Kleiner hit the fireman's second offering over the roof of the stands in right field, scoring Jorgeson ahead of him. Johnny Gramner threw a loaded bat away, swung the light one around his head as he walked to the plate. Shelby whipped two strikes by him, and then gave him a change-up. Johnny dug in and timed it right, belting it past a lunging Quaker third baseman for another double. Shelby, after a short conference with his catcher, struck out Pat O'Dowd. He got two called strikes by McHenry, then lost his control and walked him. Pete Cuzco went flat into the dirt from a duster after a ball and a strike had been called, then got up and slammed Shelby's fast ball through the middle, scoring Johnny Gramner. Shelby struck Willie Furber out when the pitcher came up for the second time. The Tanagers were leading, 6–0.

The major leaguers got two runs back in the fifth on an error by Speck Armitage and a homer by Wyrosnik, but Willie Furber held the Quakers' big guns up to the ninth. Pat O'Dowd had homered in the seventh for the Tanagers, and Willie had a five-run lead when the Phillies came in for their last turn at bat.

Mel Wessler led off and dropped a blooper into short right that Leo Kleiner tried to trap. The ball rolled by him and Wessler went to second. Willie Furber worked too carefully on O'Doul's shortstop and walked him, and then the Quaker catcher slammed one to deep short that Speck backhanded but could not throw. The bases were loaded and nobody out when one of the most murderous clutch hitters in the game stepped into the batter's box. Delennis looked at Willie's curve and at his fast ball and let both go by. Both were strikes, and the fans started talking it up.

Willie threw a blazing fast ball and Delennis nailed it into the second-base hole. Johnny Gramner raced in, backhanded the ball, stepped on second and fired to Robek. He went high into the air and came down on top of the Quaker base runner, and the racket in the stands

160

told him he'd made the double play. A run scored for the big league club, but Willie Furber still had a four-run margin. The crowd was still cheering the Gramner play when Willie got a third strike by the Quaker center fielder, ending the ball game. The minor leaguers had won it, 7–3.

In the Tanager dressing room, Leo Kleiner said, "They'll be talking about that double play for a long time in this town, Johnny."

The player grinned. He'd had three for two and a sacrifice, and four assists besides the twin killing. He'd had a whale of a good time, too, and he was proud of the Tanagers for coming out on top of the big-time team. A great gang, these Tanagers.

Willie Furber sat in front of a locker, slowly shaking his head from side to side. "Wake me up, somebody," he said. "I just dreamed I beat the Phillies with six hits."

"All right, Cinderella man, get showered," the manager said. "And don't get pumpkin heads. They could slaughter us tomorrow."

In the hotel room, Speck Armitage said, "I'm celebratin', Johnny. I'm callin' my girl. Any message for Madge?"

Johnny Gramner was living that double play over again. "Huh?" he asked.

"I'm callin' Dora. Any word for Madge?"

"Tell her not to forget to buy the Zanesport paper first thing tomorrow," Johnny said.

"A very sentimental message," Speck said and picked up the phone. A few minutes later, Speck covered the mouthpiece with his hand and turned to Johnny. "A man answered. A Dr. Norton. I—" He spoke into the phone again. "Dora? Hello, sweetheart. Sure, I'm fine. You're having a party? I can hear the racket. Madge's birthday? Well, that's great. Give her my best." He talked another couple of minutes and handed the phone to Johnny. "Talk to Madge, hot-shot. Wish her many happy returns."

The voice far away was very clear and soft in Johnny's ears. The girl said she was awfully glad to hear he was doing so well and would be glad to see him soon. And suddenly the ballplayer was at a loss for words, with a pleasant ache in his chest. After a while he said, "Happy birthday, Madge. I'll see you pretty soon."

"Mel wrote me," the girl said. "He said he had a talk with you, Johnny." She laughed. "Don't let him scare you."

"Well, maybe Dora would like to talk to Speck again," the second baseman said and handed the phone to the shortstop. His hand was shaking.

"*Some* Charles Boyer," Speck sniffed and took over.

Gaffney started DelGardo against the Quakers in the third game of the exhibition series. The major leaguers knocked the left-hander out in the bottom of the fourth with two singles, a walk, and a big triple by Wyrosnik. Harvey Drew took over and put the fire out after four runs had scored.

Johnny Gramner stepped up to the plate to lead off the inning for the Tanagers, and after he had two called strikes against him, he happened to glance toward the Philly bench. Bucky O'Doul was in front of his dugout, resting on one knee and studying him intently. He wiped a nervous hand on the front of his shirt, dug in, and waited. The pitch was over but too low. The next offering just missed the inside corner. The Quaker bench began

162

chattering, and Johnny stepped out of the batter's box to get some dirt on his hands.

The pitch came in, a blazing fast ball, and the Tanager second baseman shifted his feet and laced it into right for a single. O'Dowd popped to the third baseman, and then Johnny got the sign to start running after the count was even at two and two on Steve McHenry. McHenry swung at the next pitch, a hot grounder to deep short, and was out on a fine throw. Johnny was safe at second, defeating a possible Quaker double play. Standing on the bag, he saw that O'Doul was still in front of his dugout.

Pete Cuzco, after working the string out, hit a blooper to shallow left. Delennis came racing in to get it on the first hop, and he fired into the plate. Johnny rounded third at top speed and hit the dirt three feet from the dish, bowling over O'Doul's husky backstop, Burger. The umpire called him safe and he got up banging the dirt from his uniform, a wide grin on his face.

Drew struck out, and Zanesport took the field. The Quaker offense started clicking again, thanks to a boot by Ted Robek on a hot one near the first-base bag. Johnny kept looking toward O'Doul. He knew the big league manager's eyes were on his every move. The pressure was on him and he tried to stay loose while Wyrosnik was hitting. The heavy hitter always pulled them to the right side, and they were generally ablaze when they scorched through the infield. That is, unless he belted them out of the park.

Wyrosnik swung. The ball hit the dirt two feet to Gramner's right, and he moved fast and backhanded it, simply flipped it while off balance to Armitage, who threw to Robek for two out. A run crossed the plate, but the Quakers were robbed of a big inning. Drew, using

163

all the savvy gleaned from six years of major league pitching, got the next man to send a lazy fly to right center that was gathered in by McHenry. The crowd applauded the Tanager second baseman as he came into the dugout. Stan Coveskie said as Johnny sat down, "O'Doul's making book on you."

Johnny thought, That's O.K. I hope he keeps looking.

The Tanagers came into the first half of the eighth trailing by a score of 7–1. Jorgeson led off and struck out, but the Quaker catcher let the third strike elude him, and Jorgeson raced to first and was safe by half a step. Robek ignored two pitches, then stepped into a curve that failed to break too sharply and hit the ball down the third-base line to the Quaker bull pen. Jorgeson scored all the way from first on the double, and Robek took third with a hook slide when the Philly catcher fired the throw-in from the outfield like a bullet to the hot corner.

Leo Kleiner singled to left, scoring Robek. Johnny Gramner came up again and worked the count to two and one, then proceeded to rip a line drive past the pitcher and into center field. O'Doul took the pitcher out. An old and canny right-hander took over and struck out Steve McHenry, but Pete Cuzco drove one through the Quaker infield for another hit, and Kleiner came around. Harvey Drew fanned, ending the rally. The Quakers still led, 7–4.

O'Doul's hitters started finding Drew in their half. A hit, a walk, and a drag bunt loaded the bases with no one out. Mel Wessler hit a three-and-one pitch that arced over the infield, and it looked like two more runs to the fans in the Atlanta ball park. McHenry had no chance of catching up with it before it hit the grass, but Johnny Gramner was running at top speed, and suddenly he reached over

164

his shoulder and caught the ball, whirled, and fired to third. Jorgeson threw across the diamond to Robek for the double play. A triple killing went awry when Speck Armitage dropped Robek's peg from first.

The crowd was up and cheering the terrific catch. In front of the Quaker dugout, Bucky O'Doul stood looking at Johnny. A coach was with him, and he nodded at something O'Doul said. Harvey Drew got out of the inning unscathed when he got the next batter to hit a pop fly high to Jorgeson in foul territory. The game ended without further scoring, and the Tanagers headed for the dressing room. Their next stop would be Raleigh, North Carolina, to meet the Tarheels of the South Atlantic League.

Bucky O'Doul came into the Tanager dressing room, his big cigar belching smoke. He ribbed Mike Gaffney and Harvey Drew for a few moments, then centered his gaze upon Johnny Gramner. "Quite a ballplayer, Mike, and only a kid. Take care of that piece of property or I'll have your scalp. That's another Eddie Collins." He walked over to the Tanager infielder. "Nice goin', Johnny. You'll be playing for me some day."

Maybe, Johnny thought. How much were they paying big league second basemen? He said, "I hope so, Mr. O'Doul."

The Zanesport team arrived home with an average of twelve won and three lost in the exhibition games. It was a much stronger team than the one that had won the pennant the previous year, and the Tanager fans had purchased their tickets early for the league opener with the Lansing Senators.

But Johnny Gramner's morale got a jolt when he read

165

a letter from his mother that was waiting for him at the Fairmount Hotel. *". . . Ricky was taken to juvenile court with the others, Johnny,"* she'd written. *"But they let them off. The police claimed Ricky and the rest of that gang broke into a cigar store and stole over a hundred dollars. Ricky swears he didn't have anything to do with it, but sometimes I. . . ."*

Johnny immediately wrote two letters, one to his mother and the other to Al Sava. He asked Al to watch Ricky and keep him straight, to pin his ears back, if necessary, and he asked him for the straight dope on the so-called Black Tigers.

It occurred to him as he mailed the letter that Sava's stature had shrunk, somehow, and the thought gave him a vague feeling of disloyalty. Was Sava really the man to watch out for Rick, to keep him straight? What kind of a deal was he working with his brother? If he saw that those kids had regular jobs, why did they find it necessary to break into stores? Something smelled there, he decided. Perhaps he ought to look into it.

But Bridge City was a long way off. And he had to look out for Johnny Gramner first, didn't he?

The night before the opener with the Senators, Johnny called Madge at the hospital. She seemed genuinely pleased to hear from him, said she would be happy to see him at nine thirty, when she came off duty. Speck Armitage offered Johnny his car. "Now you're in there swinging," the shortstop said. "Never let the good ones go by, Johnny."

Madge seemed prettier than ever when he helped her into the coupé, and he was practically tongue-tied until they had driven into the countryside. "Your brother

166

hinted he would work on me if—that is—if I hurt you in any way," he blurted out. "Why would I want to do that?"

"I have no idea, Johnny," Madge said a little breathlessly. "Sometimes we hurt people without realizing it. Sometimes a situation is as one-sided as a sixteen-to-one ball game. You can't force two people to think the same way. I—"

"You must've told Mel you—you—liked me." Johnny nearly drove off the road. His heart was pounding, and he guessed his ears glowed red in the darkness.

"Yes, Johnny. I did."

"I think a lot of you, too," Johnny said, and then his tongue froze to the roof of his mouth, and he did not get it loose until they were driving back into Zanesport. "How about this Paul Norton?" he finally asked.

"He's marrying that redhead." Madge laughed.

"I never really liked that guy until now," Johnny said. Now he had two reasons to become the most valuable second baseman in any league. There was an understanding between him and Madge even though it had not actually been put into words. Johnny had never been happier in his life even though he was anything but sentimental as he said good night to Madge.

"I'll be rooting for you tomorrow, Johnny," she told him, and he watched her until she'd stepped into the self-service elevator. It was unbelievable that this could have happened to a guy from West Lancey Street.

CHAPTER 15

THE ZANESPORT FANS GOT THEIR FIRST LOOK AT Gaffney's new players the next afternoon. Steve McHenry in center field justified the hand he received by singling his first time at bat in the last of the third. The visitors had scored off Willie Furber in the second frame with a home run by Darlman, Lansing's top hitter. The farmer boy had weathered the inning, thanks to a twin killing—Armitage to Gramner to Robek. Pete Cuzco forced McHenry at second, and Speck came up and greeted Seymour, the Lansing southpaw, with a sharp drive down the third-base line for two bases. Jorgeson walked.

Ted Robek fouled two pitches off, refused to bite at Seymour's wide ones, then belted a triple to the fence in deep right. McHenry, Armitage, and Jorgeson scored. The Lansing manager walked to the mound. Seymour was replaced by a right-hander, and Leo Kleiner scored Robek with a towering fly to center. There were two out when Johnny Gramner advanced to the plate. A great stop by the Senator first baseman had robbed him of a hit in the second inning.

The crowd yelled with anticipation. Johnny looked down toward third base after fouling off the first pitch. Speck had told him that Dora and Madge would be here. He swung hard at a bad pitch, and the Lansing bench began to ride him. Gaffney called out, "Get that good pitch, Johnny."

168

The right-hander pumped twice, fired his curve in. It did not break sharply enough and the Tanager flash hit the ball into right for a single. With two out, Pat O'Dowd caught a fast one on the meat end of his bat and rode it out of the ball park. The stands were in an uproar as he scored behind Johnny. Steve McHenry came up for the second time and rolled out to the Lansing shortstop. The Tanagers took the field with a 6–1 lead.

Out on the skin part of the infield, Johnny remembered the first game he had played for Zanesport. He had been the lonesomest man in the world. Speck, a few yards away at shortstop, had been a total stranger. Johnny had been a single fish in a big glass bowl, and thousands of people, their faces looking alike under the arc lights, had screamed for him to show them why he was there. This year he felt at home. He was part of a family that was made up of Speck and Dora and Madge. The fans had accepted the fact that he was their second baseman and were giving him their heartiest support.

He had learned a lot of baseball from these Tanagers, particularly from Mike Gaffney and Sam Berman, who had been around a long time. And Pat O'Dowd, behind the plate, had maneuvered him into the correct position many times to enable him to be where a certain ball was hit. Right now Pat was signaling to him to get deeper into the hole with a dead right field hitter coming up for the Senators.

The ball came his way with smoke on it. He dug it out after running a few steps and fired to Ted Robek. The first baseman dropped the ball for an error, and the roar of the crowd suddenly broke off. Willie Furber grinned at Robek as he rubbed up the ball. Johnny yelled, "O.K., so we get two next time!"

Jenke, the Lansing hitter, worked Willie to a full count

and then belted one behind the runner into right field. The man on first scooted all the way to third. Mike Gaffney came out of the dugout and waved to his bull pen. Preacher Marcum and Harvey Drew began warming up.

Willie struck out the next hitter, and then Pat O'Dowd came out to the mound. Speck and Johnny came in from their positions to get signals straight. The batter waiting at the plate was a pull hitter to left. It meant that Speck Armitage had to play his position far from the keystone sack, so it would be impossible for him to complete his part of a double-steal defense. O'Dowd said, "Johnny, the next will be a waste pitch, so as soon as the ball passes that batter, you jump toward second base."

Johnny nodded. Sam Berman had drilled this play into him more than once. The Senators were a running team, real go-go boys, and Mike Gaffney had anticipated a double steal here.

Willie Furber threw the waste pitch, and Johnny ran to the second sack as the base runners took off. He ran in to meet O'Dowd's throw and then relayed it back to the catcher, who tagged the Lansing runner out by a foot. O'Dowd fired back to second, where Speck Armitage had taken over, but the man was in with a pretty hook slide. But with one out and only one on now, Willie Furber eased off and got the next two hitters to sky to the outfielders.

On his way to the dugout via third base, Johnny saw a girl waving to him and felt ten feet tall when he sat down alongside Speck. "They're here, Johnny," Speck told him. "Madge has a light blue coat and a little white hat."

As Pete Cuzco stepped in to hit, Johnny thought, If Al Sava could read my thoughts now! The tough kid from West Lancey with a picture of a girl inside his head, a girl with brown hair and brown eyes taking something out of an oven in a cozy apartment, waiting for a ball-player to come home.

Johnny thought it was a little crazy himself. He had to concentrate on baseball to make sure of the base hits that would assure him a bonus and keep Bucky O'Doul watching the minor league averages.

He came to bat later in the inning, with a run already across and the bases full, and hit the relief pitcher's first delivery off the Senator second baseman's glove and into right field. Armitage and Robek scored and Willie Furber had a nine-run lead. O'Dowd left two on when he skied high to the infield.

The Tanagers left town with a .778 average, in first place by three full games, having won seven and lost two. They were in Des Moines when the news broke, and repercussions were felt in every corner of the country where baseball was played. Speck Armitage brought the newspaper to the hotel room an hour after the Tanagers had left the dining room. The shortstop's face was gray. Johnny had just finished talking to Madge on the phone when Speck handed him the Des Moines *Register*. The ballplayer stared at the headlines:

"SLAIN GANGSTER EX-BIG LEAGUE BALL PLAYER
"Al Sava, Found Shot in Bridge City, Identified as Frank Crowell, Banished from Organized Ball in 1940"

171

Johnny Gramner, a terrible tightness in his chest, read the detailed story under the screaming headlines. Sava, the police discovered, had been a modern Fagin, and records he had kept in his files divulged the names of a dozen teen-agers he had used to do his petty stealing. Police had rounded up the juvenile Black Tiger gang, and all were in custody.

Johnny looked at Speck, his eyes full of shock. The shortstop's voice was scarcely audible. "Your big hero, pal. But read the next paragraph." He picked up his coat and left the room. The second baseman read further, fear heavy upon him. Letters had been found in the crook's office, and the contents of one of these proved to the district attorney beyond a doubt that a minor league ballplayer had been implicated in Sava's operations. The club owners had been notified and promised drastic action if the player's explanation was not satisfactory. Up to the time the paper had gone to press, the name of the minor leaguer had been withheld.

Johnny Gramner let the newspaper slip from his limp fingers to the floor. There was a numbness in him, a fright that brought a touch of nausea. He fought to remember what he had written to Sava, but his mind was darkly clouded. Baseball had given him everything, had taken him out of the slums, out of obscurity. It had given him confidence, and a girl like Madge. And now the bright world was crashing around him. The man who had been his best friend on the Tanager ball club had walked out of the room. Madge would certainly have the news by now and it would be easy for her to read between the lines.

What had he written? He remembered some of the things—like assuring Sava he'd get every last dollar out

172

of the game, look out for Johnny Gramner first. Things like that. They couldn't break a man for that. He was pacing the floor, still trying to remember, when there was a knock on the door. He stood very still for a moment, fearful of the identity of the person who would step into the room. Finally he said chokingly, "Come in."

Mike Gaffney closed the door softly behind him, his eyes gravely serious. "Johnny," he said, "you're on a spot." He sat down on the edge of the bed. "One time you wrote Sava, this ex-ballplayer, not to bet on the Carlton Braves. Why?"

Johnny recalled the letter now. Pleadingly he said, "Mike, I did write him that, but because I figured the Braves couldn't win without me in the line-up. It didn't mean I'd throw a game so that he could—"

"The implication is there in big black and white, Johnny," Mike said. "You've been close to one of the worst rats ever to gnaw at the game. Crowell threw games to Detroit when he was with the Chicago Bruins. The smell from him is on you. How deep were you in with that crook?"

"I knew him when I grew up in Bridge City." There were tears in Johnny's eyes. "He got me into sand-lot ball, then semipro. I thought I owed him plenty. I believed everything he told me, Mike. Well, he's put me back where I started." He dropped into a chair, buried his face in his hands.

Mike Gaffney patted him on the shoulder. "I promise to do everything I can, Johnny. If you have any friends now, you'll need them."

It all came back to the star second baseman, a not-so-dim past full of things he had neglected to do. Like thanking men like Dan Kelso and Mose Watson. Those

173

were the men he should have written to. He had been content to travel the road alone, secure in the belief that he had talent enough to see him through.

"I've been talking to the front office, Johnny." Mike Gaffney's voice sounded far away. "You are under suspension indefinitely, of course. You won't be admitted to a ball park. Tomorrow the papers will tell the fans that you're the one under suspicion. You'll have to keep your chin up."

When Gaffney went out, Johnny thought of Ricky and knew now why his mother had been frightened last Christmas. All this could have been prevented, he told himself, if he hadn't kowtowed to an idol with feet of the filthiest clay. Where could he go if they decided he was unfit to play baseball? Maybe he'd have to change his name and find himself a hole as Al Sava had done, far from people like Speck and Madge. His throat ached as he thought of her and what might easily have been, and then he threw himself down on the bed and sobbed like a grammar school kid, he was that afraid.

Johnny stayed in his room all afternoon and part of the night. Then he walked the streets that were darkest, thinking of Chico Gonzales playing the keystone sack for the Tanagers, and of the players trying to give all they had, knowing why Johnny Gramner was not in the park. Curt Simonson was pitching for Gaffney. Johnny ducked into a small cafe at the edge of Zanesport and got the seventh inning over the radio.

"That ball Gonzales missed would have been easy for Johnny Gramner. As soon as we know why the flash isn't in the line-up, we'll pass it on to you fans. Leo Kleiner steps in with two down and Jorgeson leading off second. Des Moines is out in front three to one. Benson's first

174

pitch is a ball. Kleiner hits the next pitch through—wow, the third baseman made a terrific save. He's got Jorgeson trapped. He throws to the shortstop. Frankel joins the chase along the base line. The third baseman gets the throw from the second baseman and Jorgeson is tagged out. That's all for the Tanager threat. At the end of the fourth, Lake City is leading the Omaha Packers, five to three. The Cubs come in for their cuts—"

Johnny stepped into the hotel room an hour later and found a telegram on the floor near the door. He ripped the yellow envelope open and the message said: "ARRIVE IN DES MOINES TOMORROW ELEVEN. KEEP A STIFF UPPER LIP. DAN KELSO."

Choking up again, Johnny read the words over and over. They were little lights in the darkness. Words from a friend he needed now. *Dan Kelso, batting for Gramner.* He was still sitting there, the telegram clutched in his hand, when Speck came in.

"Lost it, eight-six," the shortstop said. "How are you feeling, Johnny?"

"Scared," the second baseman said. "What are the other guys saying?"

"Not a word," Speck said. "But they don't believe there's a crooked little bone in your body. The commissioner is something else again. Man, we missed you out there."

"Thanks." Johnny wanted to ask Speck if he thought Madge knew, but his voice was breaking.

The papers carried the story in the morning. The headlines screamed: "JOHNNY GRAMNER, TANAGER SECOND BASEMAN, SUSPENDED. *Player Involved in Crowell Mess.*"

The Tanager players came to Johnny Gramner's room singly and in groups. They gave him a clean slate, assured him of their full support when the investigation came up. The phone rang when the last two players left and Johnny let it ring. A few minutes later it cut loose again and this time he picked it up. It was Madge Wessler. "Johnny, I don't believe any of it. I want you to know that, no matter what happens, you hear?"

"Yes, I do," Johnny said, his heart nearly bursting. "You're a wonderful person, Madge. I—I—"

"Stay in there and keep swinging, Johnny. Don't let a bad call get you down."

Later, the ballplayer stood by the window staring into the busy Des Moines street, convinced that he had been the wrongest guy in the world. You didn't go any place alone; you needed other people, and they needed you, he realized. It did not matter what your beginning had been, but what you made of yourself.

Stan Coveskie and Mose Watson had begun life with just as many strikes against them as Johnny had, but they'd come out on top. Maybe they didn't get the biggest salaries in the league, but they were real ballplayers, men who also played the game of life right. They'd tried to show Johnny how, and he'd refused to learn. He hoped it wasn't too late now.

Dan Kelso walked in a few minutes later. The Carlton manager gave Johnny the old broad smile, and after pumping his hand, stood back and appraised him. "Broader shoulders. You've grown two inches, Johnny. No wonder you've been hitting over three hundred."

"I'm hitting about zero now, Dan," Johnny said. "I'm sorry I didn't congratulate you winning that pennant last year. I've been a mighty cold-blooded guy. And you bothering to come here to—"

Dan Kelso sat down. "You've got friends back in Carlton, Johnny. Remember Mrs. Grady?"

Johnny nodded.

"She sent for me when she heard the news," Kelso said. "Gave me a letter she found in your room when you left. If she had turned it over to the authorities it would have murdered you, Johnny. Here, take a look at it."

It was the letter Johnny had received from Al Sava telling him he had bet some money on the Laraine Robins because Johnny seemed so certain Carlton wouldn't win the pennant. He looked at Dan Kelso, his lips trembling. "Mrs. Grady, Dan. She—"

"She liked you, Johnny. Oh, she said you were a fresh, impossible busher, but you were some ballplayer. You know this Al Sava or Frank Crowell was shot for welching on some bets. They got the two toughs that caught up with him. Got any more letters from that man in your possession?"

Johnny shook his head. "No, Dan. I was just about forgetting him entirely when this happened. You don't think for a minute I'd throw a game?"

"I'd sooner believe Goliath laid down to David, Johnny," Kelso said. "The boys back on my club sent their best wishes and will go to bat for you a hundred per cent. Mose said, 'Tell Johnny I will bring a stack of Bibles an' swear on all of 'em if they ask me questions.'"

"Mose," Johnny said softly. "A real gentleman, Dan. Whiter than I'll ever be."

Dan Kelso stayed with Johnny Gramner until late in the afternoon. Before he left to catch his train, he said, "Don't forget how serious this can be, Johnny. Circumstantial evidence is enough to convict some men, especially if they're accused of a crime against baseball.

177

The game is as much a part of this country as the Grand Canyon or the Hoover Dam, and the fans will scream for the hide of any man that tries to ruin it."

"Sure," Johnny said. "I don't blame them."

Johnny called Mike Gaffney's room after Kelso had gone. "Mike," he said, "how do I stand? I'd like to run down to Bridge City until tomorrow night to see my kid brother. He's in the jam with me."

Mike said, "This isn't 1940, Johnny. Tampering with any sport is considered a felony now. They don't just ban you from baseball. I'll call you back and let you know."

Johnny's face glistened with sweat. It could be jail. He hadn't thought of that. A bad decision and he could say good-by to everything, including Madge. He sat down and the fears rode him hard again. He started violently when the phone rang. It was Mike Gaffney. "It's all right, Johnny," he said. "They aren't throwing you in the clink yet, but you're to be back by Wednesday morning, understand?"

"Right, Mike," the ballplayer said.

CHAPTER 16

Johnny Gramner arrived in Bridge City at mid-night. His mother was still up when he walked into the dingy flat on West Lancey Street. Her face was wan, her eyes red. For the first time in many years he took her in his arms, and looked over her shoulder at Ricky Gramner, not half as big as he looked several months ago. He was, however, not fully chastened.

"So you and Al had a deal, huh?" Ricky said, and Johnny gently moved his mother away from him and walked up to his brother and yanked him to his feet.

"There's nothing to that, Rick! I had no bets with Sava! You! You went out and did his stealing for him. You lied to Ma. What did the cops find on you, a switch-blade? If they let you go, I'm taking you over, big shot! I'll knock you in line if it takes me the next ten years."

Yet Johnny knew it wasn't just a matter of knocking a brash kid into line. West Lancey had done plenty of knocking, and The Black Tigers were the result. Rick had to learn, Johnny was just beginning to recognize, that working with people was more important than fighting them—that they'd give back what you gave more often than not.

He stared into his brother's sullen eyes and for the first time knew he was the guilty one because he hadn't come home sooner to see how things were going, hadn't stuck around longer at Christmas to find out why his mother was so frightened for Rick, hadn't stood up to Al Sava and his false philosophy.

"He had a zip gun, Johnny," Mrs. Gramner said. "He was in juvenile court this morning. He was put on probation."

"Lucky," Johnny said. "Maybe luckier than I'll be." He walked to the window and looked out over the street, saw that there were twice as many bluecoats patrolling there. The Black Tigers were smashed, but a new gang could spring up. Getting caught and humiliated only made them more resentful on West Lancey. If a good man would make an experiment here, a man of the cloth, somebody, perhaps a lot of the kids could grow up to be decent men and women.

"What will they do to you, Johnny?" his mother asked.

"I don't know. A lot of people are rooting for me, Ma. Ballplayers everywhere. My girl—"

"Johnny!" his mother said, eyes brightening. "A girl? I'm glad. You need somebody to—"

Ricky said, "A dame yet!"

"Get on your feet!" Johnny's eyes were blazing.

The boy stood up. The ballplayer snapped, "You're sorry you called her that. Say it or I'll—!"

"I'm sorry," the boy said.

Johnny pushed him back into the chair. "Now listen, Ricky! I'll send you a few dollars every week as long as I hear from Mother that you deserve it. You'll go to Sunday school every week. If you miss without any good excuse, you'll get a thrashing from me for every one of them. Ma will keep the score. If you ever join up with another gang of punks, I'll come down here and clean you all up with a baseball bat!"

Ricky Gramner nodded his head, reached for a comic magazine. Johnny ripped it out of his hand and glanced at the title. *Crime Wave Comics*. He ripped it up and fired it into a wastebasket. "If I find out you're buying this junk with my money, you'll never get another nickel. That plain enough?"

Threatening Rick like this wasn't the real answer, Johnny knew, but right now the kid needed something to knock a little sense into him.

Ricky, all the cockiness out of him now, nodded his head again.

Johnny slept well that night, everything considered.

180

After breakfast he took his brother aside. "You had it comin', Rick. You and me both. How about it? Let's start all over. O.K.?"

The boy hesitated, suddenly grinned sheepishly. "O.K., Johnny. It's a deal."

He walked halfway to school with Rick. On the way back he bought the Bridge City papers. A front page story said that all the Carlton players would swear by Johnny Gramner. Dan Kelso had been quoted. *"The charges against Johnny Gramner are baseless! Every ballplayer on every club he played against in this league will swear to that. He never knew who Al Sava really was."*

If only Rick and every other kid on West Lancey could have a friend like Dan Kelso, Johnny thought. No matter what happened, he realized, he'd learned something pretty important about people from this thing—even if it didn't boost his batting average or improve his contract terms.

Johnny walked the neighborhood for the rest of the day, and several times he was mobbed by groups of wide-eyed small fry asking for his autograph. He passed by a big policeman he had cause to remember, and the cop said, "Johnny, you look fine, you do. An' I don't believe a word of it."

"Thanks, Reilly." Johnny grinned. "I used to get in your hair."

"A little, I admit. But you were easy to comb out, Johnny. I wish you the best of luck."

He put in a call to Mike Gaffney in Omaha and was instructed to return to Zanesport. No date had been set for the preliminary hearing, the manager said, and asked how he'd found things in his home town.

"I think everything is fine here now, Mike," Johnny

181

said. "It's an ill wind and all that, as they say. Who you pitching against the Packers tonight?"

"Stan Coveskie," Mike said. "It hasn't been good so far. The Cubs took two out of three from us in Des Moines. Take it easy, Johnny. I think we can lick this thing."

Johnny took the train for Zanesport, thinking of people like Dan Kelso, Mrs. Grady, Mose Watson, and all the others who were sticking by him, and looked back to a resentful, arrogant busher taking a bus out of Carlton. It did not seem possible he had been that man. If he had been Madge that day, he would have forgotten to be a lady.

Across the aisle a man said to a companion, "What do you think of this Gramner thing, Ed?"

"Sounds whacky to me," the other man said. "But you never know. A youngster gets mixed up with the wrong people and he's tarred with the same brush. I sure hope he's cleared."

The ballplayer slumped down in his seat and made himself as inconspicuous as possible. Sure, he told himself, he'd found this to be a pretty fair sort of world the last few days.

Three days later he was notified that he was to report to the office of the league president, Frank Johnson, in Youngstown. A wire arrived almost simultaneously from Mike Gaffney telling Johnny he'd see him at the hotel in Youngstown as soon as possible after his plane landed. That morning the Tanager second baseman had read that Forbes Landrick, baseball's high commissioner, was confined to his bed with influenza. Landrick, however, was following the Gramner case with the utmost interest.

Mike Gaffney walked into Johnny's room at the hotel

182

at eleven o'clock on the eventful day. The manager's rugged face was beaming, although the Tanagers had done no better than break even on the current road trip. Mike said, "You're a lucky stiff, Johnny," after shaking hands. "You've got it beat if what I hear is true. Dan Kelso and Huck Ryerson, manager of the Laraine club, went to see Landrick personally. I understand the commissioner has communicated with Frank Johnson. Talked to a couple of baseball writers on the plane. Hundreds of letters have poured in from ballplayers and fans all over this part of the country. Who are you anyway?"

"I don't deserve it," Johnny said, and knew that one person whose name would never get in print had really made the greatest assist—Mrs. Grady. Come what may, he'd surely let her know he was grateful.

"There'll be no indictments if Johnson is satisfied," Gaffney said, and set off a fresh cigar. "When you talk to him don't spare yourself, Johnny."

At two o'clock that afternoon, Johnny Gramner ran the gantlet of sportswriters as he moved along a corridor of the Fisk Building with Mike Gaffney. They began to fire questions and the Tanager manager growled, "Not yet, boys. You know better than that!"

Johnny grinned. "Go find a man biting a dog."

"A sense of humor?" a writer gasped. "Where did he get that?"

Johnny Gramner sat at the league president's desk a few minutes later and told his story, giving himself none the best of it. The man he'd known as Al Sava had filled him full of wrong ideas. Kids in that neighborhood in Bridge City were born with chips on their shoulders. "I meant nothing in that letter you have on your desk, sir. Mike Gaffney and Dan Kelso and a lot of other people

183

will tell you what a fatheaded rookie I was. I thought I was the whole ball club. They couldn't do without me. And I honestly thought that when I was sold to the Zanesport club, Carlton couldn't possibly beat the Laraine Robins to the pennant."

President Johnson studied Johnny's face for several moments, glanced toward Gaffney, and smiled a little. "I have a detailed account from Commissioner Landrick," he said. "In it the manager of the Laraine club has a report on your playing against his team. You hit four twenty-four against his pitchers, and fielded like a Billy Martin. There is no evidence anywhere that you ever put yourself under wraps. You thought you owed this man who called himself Al Sava a favor. That correct, Gramner?"

"It is, sir," Johnny said. "He told me in his letters he was betting on the Braves. As I said, without me I didn't think Carlton would win. I deserve to get booted out for making such a dumb play, sir. I thought I knew everything. I wouldn't listen to people with brains."

"Ever bet on a professional ball game, Gramner?"

Johnny shook his head. "Once I almost did, but Kelso found it out and nearly threw me back to the sand-lots."

The league president picked up the long, typewritten letter from the commissioner and read a few paragraphs. Johnny sat tensely in his chair. Mike Gaffney leaned forward, his slouch hat hanging from his fingers. Beads of perspiration began to glisten on his forehead.

The president cleared his throat and put the letter aside. "Gramner, Mr. Landrick sees no reason to carry this case any farther. There's no evidence that you have committed any great wrong. We know that there are two kinds of errors made in baseball. Errors of commission

184

and errors of omission. You're a little guilty of making the second variety. A mountain can be made out of a molehill, remember that, Gramner. You will be reinstated immediately."

He got up and held out his hand. Johnny arose and tried to control the big lump in his throat. "Thank you, sir. I'll never forget this, Mr. Johnson."

Mike Gaffney growled, "See that you don't, Johnny! Get on your knees every night before you hit the sack and say a prayer." The manager reached for the president's hand. "Remember when you wrote for the Detroit *Tribune,* Frank? You called me the worst pop-off in the game? The best minor league player in the majors?"

"Sure, Mike," Johnson grinned. "Weren't those the days?"

The writers mobbed Mike Gaffney and his star second baseman when they emerged from the president's office. Johnny, walking on big fleecy clouds, told them all they wanted to know. One writer asked, "Is it true you're engaged to a girl in Zanesport? What's her name, Johnny?"

"Madge," Johnny said, his tongue running wild. "Madge Wessler."

"Any relation to Mel Wessler of the Quakers?"

"Sister," Johnny said, and Mike Gaffney grabbed him and shoved him into the elevator.

Back at the hotel, Mike Gaffney eyed Johnny with mixed emotions. "Now that you're almost rational, Johnny, was that true about you and—?"

"Oh, golly," Johnny said and clamped his hands to his head. "I never asked her, Mike."

Gaffney got a cigar burning, grinned through the smoke at his second baseman. "Well, you get out of one

185

mess, kid, then jump into another. You could easily get shot. Pack up fast. You can get into tonight's game in Topeka and get us out of the slump. There's a plane out in about half an hour. She'll probably hit the ceiling, you knucklehead."

"Not her," Johnny said. "She's the most wonderful girl in all the—"

"They all are," Mike said. "Get the lead out, Johnny."

Speck Armitage was the first Tanager player to reach Johnny when he walked into the visiting team's dressing room at the Topeka ball park. He threw his arms around the keystone flash and wrestled him around. All the others moved in with congratulations and good-natured ribbing. "Now we win for a change," Leo Kleiner yelled and yanked Chico Gonzales' cap down over his eyes. "Pitch anybody tonight, Mike, even Sam Berman. It'll make no difference."

Johnny suited up, sure that he would not change jobs with anyone at the moment. This was the whole world here. The sounds and the smells and the racket of the crowd overhead. Speck sidled up to him. "See Madge back there, Johnny?"

"Huh?" Johnny was suddenly scared again. "No, Speck, but I certainly will when we get home." He prayed that the writers would forget what he'd said, but knew they would not. He was the important baseball news right now. The teletypes would be clicking, and tomorrow in Zanesport, the morning papers— He pocketed his glove and followed the players out to the runway leading to the dugout, and the cries of refreshment venders were music to his ears. The Redskins' tepee was filling fast while the Tanagers took infield practice, and to Johnny

186

Gramner it was the brightest spot in the universe. A trio of Topeka players met him as he trotted back to his bench and congratulated him and wished him well.

Later, the loud-speaker announced the line-ups for the night and a tremendous roar boiled out of the stands when the announcer bawled, "At second base for the Tanagers, Johnny Gramner."

The photographers crowded the Zanesport dugout. Gaffney finally had to get tough and chase them away. Curt Simonson, unable to finish his last start, warmed up for the Tanagers, and the Redskins had a tall left-hander loosening up. At eight fifteen Speck Armitage stepped up to the plate to lead off for Gaffney. He dropped the second pitch down the third-base line, and it had English on it. It might have rolled foul if the eager Redskin third baseman had left it alone, but he picked the ball up and threw high to first and drew the first baseman off the bag.

Jorgeson came up and took two called strikes, worked the count even, and then laced one through the box for a single. A pitcher began warming up in the Redskin bull pen. The southpaw, Aloyas, bore down and got the hard-hitting Robek to slam one on the ground to the Topeka third baseman. The throw forced Jorgeson at second, but Robek beat the second baseman's peg to the initial sack. Leo Kleiner walked on four pitches, and then the crowd applauded Johnny Gramner as he dug in and faced Aloyas.

Johnny had never wanted to make a hit as much as he did now. It would be the best way to thank Mike and the Tanagers for their belief in him. Aloyas threw him a jug-handled curve that missed the outside corner, and his second pitch was high and inside. Johnny watched a strike go by, then refused to bite at one low and out-side. He looked up the line at Mike Gaffney and got the nod to hit the three-and-one pitch. It came in blazing fast. He took a healthy cut and drove it into right field close to the line. Speck and Leo Kleiner scored, and Johnny stood on the middle sack and watched the Topeka manager stride to the mound to talk to the southpaw. Pat O'Dowd hit the first pitch into shallow center field and Johnny raced in, hitting the dirt ten feet from the plate and sliding in for the Tanager's third run.

A big right-hander came in for Aloyas. He struck Steve McHenry out, and Zanesport took the field.

Curt Simonson set the Topekans down in order. After the Tanagers had picked up another run in the second on a homer by Pete Cuzco, Simonson lost his control and walked two men in a row. Waldeski, a power hitter, swung at the first pitch and sent it screaming between first and second, and the crowd rose when Johnny Gramner leaped high and pulled it down. His throw to Robek nipped the runner trying to get back, and two were out. The pitcher looked at Johnny and grinned. The runner off second said to Speck, "That was highway robbery!"

Simonson got out of the inning. The game went into the seventh with the score still 3–0 in favor of the Tanagers. Johnny Gramner led off and punched his third straight hit into right field. O'Dowd and McHenry popped out to the Redskin infield, but Cuzco, currently on a streak, caught a gopher ball on the end of his big bat and propelled it into the stands. Simonson fanned.

The Redskins nearly tore up the corn patch in the last of the ninth. A low throw from short gave the first man up a life. A six-foot, four-inch pinch hitter batted for the Redskin hurler and drove one against the center-field fence for two bases, and a run scored. Simonson walked the Topeka lead-off man and nicked the next batter on the sleeve with an inside pitch. With the bases loaded, Gaffney walked out to the center of the diamond. He called for Harvey Drew.

After a few warmup pitches, Drew was ready. The hitter dug in at the plate, and the Tanager infield moved in for a play at home base. The batter swung on the fireman's third pitch and rifled it at Johnny Gramner. The second baseman nailed it inches from the ground and fired it to Jorgeson at third. The runner slid back in, but the umpire called him out, and now there were two out and only two on. The crowd was still talking up that play Gramner had made while Harvey Drew got the last batter to sky to Cuzco in deep left.

During the next twenty-four hours, the sports pages of the newspapers around the circuit were filled with Johnny Gramner's vindication and his subsequent sensational return to the Tanager line-up. It was the Consolidated Press story that put the butterflies in Johnny's stomach. The romantic angle had been embellished, and one headline in particular caught Speck Armitage's eye as he passed a newsstand. "CUPID TAGS OUT TANAGER FLASH!" The shortstop bought a paper and ran most of the way to the hotel, where he held it close to Johnny's face.

"The whole world knows it. Does Madge?" Speck yelped.

Johnny shook his head. "Speck, I was so happy that day I didn't know what I was saying. But don't get me wrong. I want it to be this way!"

189

The shortstop grinned, took a long deep breath. "That's all I want to know, Johnny. She'll only be hoppin' mad for a while. We'll be back in Zanesport in about three days and—"

The phone rang. Speck answered it and turned a little gray. "Yeah, he's here. Oh, I'm O.K. Wait, I'll put him on." The shortstop buried the phone in a pillow and turned to the second baseman. "It—it's Madge, Johnny."

The ballplayer swallowed hard, his eyes like those of a startled deer. "Speck, tell her I've just left. I went—"

"I will not, Romeo. Talk to her."

Johnny picked up the phone and croaked, "H-hello. This is Johnny G—"

"Johnny Gramner, I want you to explain all these things in the newspapers!" Madge snapped. "I'm waiting!"

"Look, Madge," Johnny said. "It was a mistake. I'll tell them that. Tomorrow I'll give the writers a denial and—"

"You will wha–a–at?" the girl called back. "If you do, Johnny Gramner, I'll never speak to you again!"

"Madge, I don't get it. I—!" And then he knew she'd banged the phone down back in Zanesport, and he cradled the one he held and turned around and stared at Speck. He grinned wide. "Boy, she is sure something!" he said. "I can't wait until I get back."

CHAPTER 17

THREE HOURS AFTER THE BALL CLUB PILED OFF THE train, Johnny Gramner sat in the reception room of Union Hospital in Zanesport waiting for Madge to come off duty. It was midnight when she appeared, and Johnny, his heart pounding like thousands of feet that try to rattle a pitcher, got up and walked toward her. He never imagined it would be like this. Madge was smiling when she came up to him and it seemed natural to put his arms around her and hold her close. Finally she said, "Johnny, that was the craziest way to get engaged! But I know you wouldn't have had the nerve to do it any other way."

The ballplayer laughed. "I think you're right, Madge. You're not mad any more?"

"I never was. You know you haven't kissed me yet, Johnny. You can't do that through the Consolidated Press."

A few moments later he was glad he couldn't. They walked out of the hospital to join Speck and his girl. Johnny said, "Let's take a bus. It's kind of an anniversary."

The Tanagers ran wild against the league, putting on a twelve-game winning streak, and Johnny Gramner was hitting .372 when the team went on the road. They kept up a terrific .751 pace through June and July and were in front of second-place Youngstown by seven full games when the news came to the dressing room at Lake City that the Quakers of the National league were thinking of bringing Johnny Gramner up. The Philly second baseman was on the downward path, hitting only .247, and this was the year the Quakers had a chance at the flag, trailing the Brooklyn Bums by only four and a half games.

Johnny was sitting in front of his locker reading a letter from Mrs. Grady when the rumor cut through the room. He'd written his old landlady, thanking her for what she had done and promising to visit her when the season was over.

"If they want him, they get him," Mike Gaffney said to the Zanesport writers. "We'll just have to insist on a good man to take his place."

"Eighty-one runs batted in," a writer said. "You *will* miss him, Mike."

"I could insist they hold off for a few weeks," the manager said, "but the front office has something to say about it. And Johnny belongs up in the big time."

"We'll get three players for him," Berman said. "Maybe we'll about break even, Mike."

Speck sat down beside Johnny. "So you're on your way soon, big shot. How does it feel to have a big league team angle for you?"

"I can't believe it," Johnny said. "This is the chance I've dreamed about and I'm going to play it for all it's worth."

The shortstop's smile faded. "You've got a short memory," he said stiffly.

"You've got me wrong," Johnny began. "It's like this

192

—" But Speck had moved away. Maybe it was just as well not to try to explain things to everyone yet. People might get suspicious of his motives. Dan Kelso knew his plans and approved of them. That was enough.

The pot kept boiling. Zanesport fans began to write in protests against the Quaker's proposed grab of their favorite ballplayer. Rumor had it that the St. Louis Bengals were offering a hundred thousand dollars for Johnny Gramner. The second baseman, bewildered about it all, went to see Mike Gaffney in his hotel room at Covington.

"I don't know anything about baseball trading, Mike," Johnny said. "Does the Philly ball club own me?"

Gaffney shook his head. "Not entirely, Johnny. We've always called it the parent club because we have a working agreement with the Quakers. A few years back, when the club was in the second division most of the time, they came up with some financial help. Why bother your head about this inside business, Johnny?"

"If I go to the Quakers, Mike, my salary automatically goes up?" the second baseman asked.

Gaffney gave his star player a jaundiced look.

"Sure, Johnny," Mike said, hoping that what he was thinking was entirely wrong. "You could put the pressure on the Quaker front office. You're the best prospect to come out of the minor leagues since Gehringer, and if the Quakers won't give you what you want, half a dozen other clubs will grab you. You hold the reins, kid, and you have a chance to crack the whip."

"Yeah," Johnny Gramner said.

The Tanagers were at home starting a three-game series with the Omaha Packers when the wire came to the Zanesport front office. The Quakers had dropped

193

behind another two games and they needed bolstering, so they offered a pitcher, an infielder, and fifty thousand dollars for the immediate delivery of Johnny Gramner. They wanted him to report in St. Louis, where the Philadelphians played the Bengals, before the week was up.

Mike Gaffney consulted with the general manager of the Zanesport club, and a call was put through to Philadelphia to tell the Quaker organization that the deal was not that simple. Gramner knew how much he was worth, and the contract he'd signed for the Tanagers was flexible. They had better send a representative to Zanesport to discuss the deal more thoroughly.

That night, under the lights, Johnny Gramner's three hits made the difference when the Tanagers beat the Covington Browns, 3–1. He'd been in the middle of two double plays that had saved ticklish situations for Stan Coveskie. Afterward, in the locker room, Johnny was aware of a certain reserve on the part of the Tanager players; he wondered if most of them were thinking of a line in a popular sports column. *The frayed cloak of humility—how quickly it is cast aside for the velvet cloak of opulence!"*

On the way to the hotel, Speck said, "You're the luckiest stiff in the world, Johnny. Don't louse it up."

"If you were in my place, Speck," the second baseman said, "would you ask for what you figured you were worth? Look, I've got responsibilities now. There's Madge and—"

"But after that Sava business, the way they all backed you up—" Speck said. "Now you're making no secret of the fact that you're squeezing the Quaker club."

"I've got a good reason," Johnny said. "Let it go at that, Speck."

Twenty-four hours later, Johnny Gramner turned in his Tanager uniforms. The news was on the streets that the second baseman was now the property of the Philadelphia Quakers. Johnny's salary was rumored to be in excess of ten thousand dollars. The most widely read sportswriter in the midwest hinted that the Tanager flash had demanded a part of the purchase price, and opined that the Quakers still had a bargain. Their infield defense would be strengthened fifty percent, and their offensive power would equal any other in the National League.

The Tanager players gave Johnny a party at the Fairmount Hotel the night before he was to leave for St. Louis to join the Phillies. They presented him with a set of luggage and a wrist watch. Mike Gaffney said, when he made the presentation, "Never forget the old friends, Johnny. You need them on the way down the hill. You know we're gettin' a pretty good deal, boys. Two experienced major leaguers for a busher."

Johnny joined in the laughter, but the lump in his throat kept getting bigger. Leaving this ball club was not as easy as he'd anticipated, and the thrill of reaching the top had been exaggerated in his mind. When he got to his feet to make his speech, his eyes were filling and for a few long moments he struggled to find the right words.

"You're all wonderful guys," the ballplayer said. "I wish—you—were going with me. All that I can say is— thanks for everything. And you can win the pennant again—without me."

Johnny sought out Mike Gaffney before he left the

hotel with Speck. "I'll never play for a nicer guy, Mike."

"Thanks, Johnny. Make me look good up there. You know I was supposed to have developed you," Mike said. "I could be a big league manager some day."

"I'll try," the second baseman said.

He went over to the apartment house with Speck for another farewell party. When it was over, Madge said, "Johnny, keep those feet on the ground, and remember this—I don't need diamonds and mink coats, so don't try too fast for Bucky O'Doul's job. And give my love to Mel."

"Think he'll give me the lumps, Madge?" Johnny asked, a big grin on his face.

"If you find some girl and leave me in the minors, Johnny, yes." She stood on her toes for his kiss, then pushed him gently toward the door. "The best of luck, big man!"

Johnny Gramner came into the Quaker dressing room at the Bengals ball park with Bucky O'Doul an hour before the afternoon game that opened a four-game series. The manager introduced him, and when Johnny shook hands with Mel Wessler, the first baseman called out, "Take care of this busher. He's going to be my brother-in-law!"

The noise outside was like the distant beat of the surf against a shore. All the players looked big in their uniforms with the deep red piping, and Johnny felt the nervousness in his legs. The Quakers were storming toward second place and the papers that morning hoped he would be the extra stimulus the club needed.

Wyrosnik—he had cause to remember the slugger—

grinned at him. Wick Ferrill, the pitcher, said, "I hope you stick around, Johnny."

It was a strong club: Gilbeau and Hume catching; Mel Wessler at first base; Murdock and Gramner alternating at second; Rosch at short; Stu Avery at third base; Frohme, Wyrosnik, and Delennis in the outfield. Carlos Carrero, Sam Judson, Strenk, and Dick Mogridge were the right-handed pitchers. The lefties were Wick Ferrill, Lou Shelby, Red Abor, and Jim Norben. The bench was fairly strong.

When the Quakers filled the dugout on the third-base side of the diamond, Johnny looked at the crowd, the largest he had ever seen in a ball park, and the noisiest. A few minutes later he felt relieved when he learned he was not in the starting line-up. O'Doul sent Red Abor out to warm up with the bull-pen catcher, while Johnny sat on the bench next to Carrero and watched the Bengals take infield practice. The stands kept filling and the racket built up. There was a lot of chatter around him, but it failed to register. The surroundings were almost in the abstract. They were part of the kind of dream that rarely came true.

Sam Judson went out to loosen up when O'Doul decided that Abor didn't look right. Time dragged, and Johnny Gramner felt like a minnow in a deep green sea. Then Chuck Rosch, team captain, took O'Doul's batting order to the umpires waiting at the plate, and groundkeepers were dragging the infield. Back of first base, the St. Louis right-hander, Hi Noonan, was blazing them in.

Johnny got up from the bench and removed his cap when they played the National Anthem, then settled back to watch Chuck Rosch carry his bat up to the plate. In the batter's circle, Tip Murdock waited for his cut.

Noonan fired a strike across. He pushed Rosch away with one close to the letters, then threw a change-up that the lead-off man belted to deep short. The St. Louis infielder dug it out and threw the fast runner out. Johnny watched Murdock closely. This was the man playing second base for O'Doul. Murdock swung at two pitches, then was called out looking at Noonan's curve. Eddie Wyrosnik, the league's leading hitter, slammed the first pitch to deep right for two bases, but Delennis, after fouling one over the roof, rolled weakly to the box.

Judson put the Bengals down in order. The game went into the fifth inning scoreless. Murdock led off for O'Doul and fouled out to the third baseman. Wyrosnik got his second hit, and was brought all the way around when Delennis tripled inside the left-field foul line. Wessler brought the center fielder in with a towering fly to right, and then Frohme and Gilbeau grounded to the infield.

In their half the Bengals evened it up at 2–2 with a base on balls and a homer by their big first baseman, Verban. They pulled ahead in the sixth with two more runs and got Judson out. O'Doul brought in Lou Shelby, who put out the fire. He sent in Kelmer, a pinch hitter, to hit for Shelby when the Quakers came in for their cuts. The man crowded the plate and finally worked Noonan for a walk. O'Doul had Rosch swinging away, and after the count had evened, the lead-off man smashed a hit past the first baseman, and Kelmer ran to third.

"Gramner," O'Doul said. "Grab yourself a bat!"

Weak in the knees, Johnny went to the batrack. The umpire was looking toward the Quaker bench. The announcer bawled out, "Gramner—hitting for Murdock!"

198

The crowd of over seventeen thousand let out a roar that sent the shivers up Johnny's spine. The St. Louis bench laced into him as he stepped into the batter's box. "Well, well." The Bengal catcher grinned. "The flash from Zanesport!"

The fans kept up a steady racket, and out of a delegation of kids in the upper stands came the old cry, "We want a hit! We want a hit!"

Noonan bent forward, glowering at the newcomer to the majors. He fired in a fast ball that was low, but Johnny swung at it and missed it by a foot. The fans hooted, and the St. Louis bench showed him no mercy. He set his teeth and dug in, trying to make believe this was Zanesport and he was hitting against minor league stuff. Noonan gave him a curve that he watched go by and it was strike two. Off third base the Quaker coach was clapping his hands. "Get a good ball, Johnny!"

The voice sounded like Mike Gaffney's. Johnny Gramner let two more pitches go by, and then Noonan blazed it in, a little better than knee high. Johnny gave it a full cut and drove it high and far against the scoreboard. Kelmer and Rosch scored and Johnny stood at second base. This hit had drained most of the timidity out of him, and he was tingling through and through at the uproar from the stands. The score was tied. Wyrosnik worked the count to one and two, then belted a pitch through the middle to score Johnny. The Quaker players thumped Johnny on the back when he came to the dugout. "That's my boy!" Bucky O'Doul said, grinning wide.

A new pitcher came in to face Delennis. He struck the big man out, then got Mel Wessler and Frohme to fly to the outfield. Johnny Gramner took over at second base. He made a nice stop on a ball hit to his right and a prettier throw to Wessler at first to retire the first St. Louis hitter. Dick Mogridge was on the mound now for the Quakers; he looked at Johnny as he rubbed up a new ball and seemed to approve of what he saw.

O'Doul put a shift on for the powerful hitter up at the plate, and Johnny moved toward right another couple of yards.

The batter swung at Mogridge's first pitch and grounded it inside the first sack. Mel Wessler, playing close to the bag, made a frantic effort to stop it, but slipped and fell. Johnny Gramner, running hard, made the stop on the outfield grass, whirled, and threw off balance to Mogridge, covering first. The play brought the crowd up screaming. The runner was out by half a step, and the umpire's call brought half the St. Louis club down upon the arbiter's neck.

The decision stood. When play was resumed, Mogridge struck the next hitter out. Johnny ran toward the dugout amid a rousing burst of applause from the fans.

The Quakers walked off with the 5–4 ball game, and in the dressing room the writers mobbed Johnny. One said, "A pretty snappy beginning, Gramner. Makes you feel pretty good?"

"It's what they pay me for," Johnny mumbled.

"I hear it's plenty, Gramner."

"It's enough," Johnny shot back, and headed for the shower.

"Until when, Gramner?"

"You're getting a little sarcastic," the ballplayer said. "This isn't a quiz program." He went on his way.

The St. Louis writers devoted a lot of their copy to Johnny Gramner that night. In the morning the fans were reading that the new Quaker second baseman was every bit as good as the scouts said he was, and that Johnny Gramner knew it. He was a businessman besides and was going to make baseball pay off. He was the Philly club's golden boy, a serious-minded youth. In short, he was not a player to get too deep into the hearts of the fans.

Johnny tossed the papers aside, and Ollie Trimmer, a utility infielder sharing the hotel room, eyed him with interest. "They'll keep riding you, Gramner, if you rub their fur the wrong way. Those writers can put you on the skids if you don't handle 'em right."

"I never worried too much about what they thought," Johnny said, and started a letter to Dan Kelso.

The Quaker team came east only two games out of first place to show Johnny Gramner to the home-town fans. The second baseman, since taking over at the key-stone sack for O'Doul, was hitting a torrid .387. His play in the field had rock-ribbed the Philly defense. The players on the team had stamped him a real major league ballplayer, but were reserving judgment otherwise. Mel Wessler dropped into the Pullman seat next to Johnny on the way east from Chicago.

"What's the score, Johnny?" the first baseman asked. "You never spend a dime. A ten-cent limit in a poker game is too high for you. You refused to ante up a ten-dollar bill to help out a sick groundkeeper's family. I don't think that's the kind of guy Madge really went for."

"I didn't refuse to give to that guy," Johnny said. "I told Bucky O'Doul I'd owe it to him. Soon as I got my pay check, Mel. Anyway, it's nobody's business what I do."

"The writers call you a tightwad, Johnny. A guy hungry for a buck. The players can't figure you out. They want to like you, but you're making it tough for them."

"I'm playing ball for the Quakers," Johnny retorted. "That's all I was brought up to do, not to be a social lion, the life of the party."

"O.K.," Mel said, and got up and walked to the grill car.

CHAPTER 18

JOHNNY GRAMNER, MAKING HIS FIRST APPEARANCE in Philadelphia, hit a single and a home run and turned in several sparkling plays in the field. A lot of boos punctuated the applause he drew, for that morning a sports columnist had written that the flash from Zanesport was not exactly worshipped by his fellow players.

A letter came from Madge that disturbed Johnny. She wrote: "... *I can't understand all I've been seeing in the papers, Johnny. I thought you'd realize, after that mess you got out of, that you couldn't go back to being that man I met on the bus. If you are, I'm afraid I can't go along with you. I must see you and talk to you before I make any decision. ...*"

The ballplayer crumpled the letter and shoved it into his pocket, and knew the price of doing something straight from the heart, and not for the publicity gained.

The adverse publicity was bound to affect Johnny Gramner's playing. He went fourteen for nothing at the plate in the important series with the Cincinnati Braves, and booted one of the games away. Bucky O'Doul benched him in favor of Murdock, and the writers yelled that Johnny Gramner could be a flash in the pan.

He sat on the bench and watched the Brooklyns take two out of three from the Quakers and drop them back into second place. He hadn't heard from Madge in over a week, and there was a gnawing emptiness in his meridian. After the third game, taken by the Braves by the lopsided score of 12–5, the Quaker dressing room was gloomy and on edge. Bucky O'Doul was storming, and Eddie Wyrosnik snapped, "Buy a second baseman, Bucky. You got a twenty-four carat bust sitting on the bench!"

Johnny Gramner jumped to his feet and three players ganged up on him. Mel Wessler said, "Is he far wrong, Gramner?"

"Guess not," Johnny said. "Let me out of here."

At eleven o'clock the next morning, Bucky O'Doul answered a knock on the door of his room. "Come in!" he growled, and hoped it was a visitor he could cut loose on. The man came in and said, "Mr. O'Doul, I'm Dan Kelso. I used to manage Johnny Gramner."

"Yeah? I wish you had him now, Kelso."

"O'Doul, I'm here to tell you and show you something," Kelso said. "But I want the Philadelphia writers here. The guy that travels with the Quakers. Gramner is a stubborn kid. He made me promise something, O'Doul, but I'm breaking it. Take a look at this." He handed the manager a photograph.

O'Doul looked at it, puzzled. "What in blazes is it?"

"The bowling alley that crook, Crowell, ran, O'Doul,"

203

Kelso said. "The man who called himself Al Sava. Johnny Gramner came from that neighborhood, and after he was cleared of those charges, he came to me and asked me to buy that building. He bought it after he'd signed with your ball club, and it cost him twenty-eight thousand dollars. He'll be in hock for a couple of years. That's why he struck a hard bargain, O'Doul. That's the answer to a lot of things. That building is going to be used for a youth center in Bridge City."

Bucky O'Doul said, "Why didn't he say so, Kelso?"

"He figured the wolves would call it a publicity stunt —to build himself up," Kelso said. "You know how they work on a man."

O'Doul picked up the photograph again. He dropped it, turned to the phone. He called every local newspaper and talked to the men he wanted. When he was through he turned to Dan Kelso. "The story and the picture will be in every paper in the city tomorrow. Quite a boy, this Johnny Gramner."

"Bigger than you think, O'Doul. You have never been to West Lancey Street in Bridge City."

Dan Kelso left the room when the sports writers arrived.

The story hit the late editions, a few hours before the Quakers met the invading New York Titans for a night game. Mel Wessler broke into Johnny's room, a newspaper in his hand. He stopped and looked hard at the ballplayer, who jumped up from his bed. "You let us think you were a wrong character, Johnny! Don't you ever think of anybody but yourself?" He suddenly laughed. "What a crack to make after reading this sheet." He fired the newspaper at the second baseman.

Johnny read the story, slowly folded the paper and

threw it onto the dresser. "I don't know. I thought I owed a lot to the kids back there, a lot of other people. I didn't want to make a big deal out of it. I—"

They kept coming in, O'Doul, Frohme, Wyrosnik, and several others. Wyrosnik laughed. "Old John Draper, owner of this club, is goin' to get quite a boot out of this, Johnny. Said you held him up like you had a gun. You playin' tonight, Johnny?"

"He is," Bucky O'Doul said. "Imagine a modest guy like this on the Quakers."

Mel Wessler picked up Johnny's phone. He called Union Hospital in Zanesport. Johnny heard him talking to Madge and his heart got twice its size. "Read the papers early in the morning, Toots," Mel said. "You don't know what kind of a guy you got for yourself. He's a philanthropist and a civic leader. He's got rocks in his head, Madge."

Johnny Gramner trotted out to second base when the Quakers took the field that night. The ball park was two-thirds filled, and they greeted the Zanesport flash with a thundering ovation. A few minutes later, after the visitors were retired, he stepped up to the plate and singled sharply to left, stretching it to two bases when the New York left fielder failed to pick the ball up cleanly. Eddie Wyrosnik promptly hit a two-and-one pitch out of the ball park and the Quakers were off and running once more. Delennis and Mel Wessler singled back to back, and the New York pitcher was taken out. The Quakers ran onto the field with a 5–0 lead.

In the last of the seventh, Johnny stopped the first hitter's bid for a single deep on the grass and threw him out. He went back to his position, forgetting the three hits he'd made and the stab of a line drive that had saved two runs. His thoughts were back on a bus coming out of Carlton, the day he'd really started to live. And then they went back to West Lancey Street and the changes that were being made there.

He came back quickly to the game when the New York catcher belted one of Wick Ferrill's serves against the right-field fence for two bases. A pinch hitter stepped up and Ferrill worked on him carefully, too carefully. Two were on, with the head of the batting order coming up.

Johnny, as the lead-off man swung and missed Ferrill's first pitch, could hear the soft voice of Mose Watson, the veteran Carlton pitcher, and the good-natured griping of Mrs. Grady. He looked up at the arc lights and saw many faces there he hoped he could always remember.

Crack! At once he was alert. He saw the ball glance off Ferrill's glove and trickle toward the keystone sack, and he raced in and scooped it up. His quick throw was into the dirt, but Mel Wessler dug it out and got the runner by a step. The crowd let loose its roar of approval. Two were gone, but there were men on second and third.

The West Lancey Street Youth Center. It was a good name. They'd have a gym in the not-so-distant future, fully equipped. They'd most certainly have a baseball team, and kids like Rick would have a chance to get into the Little League.

The New York batter caught hold of Wick Ferrill's full-count pitch, and the ball was coming his way again, scorching the grass. He knocked it down, picked it up, and blazed it to Wessler. The throw was ahead of the runner, and the Quakers went into their dugout.

Johnny watched the Quaker hitters go up and take their cuts, and thought of the telegram he'd received an

206

hour before the game. The message read: "YOU WONDER-FUL GUY. LOVE MADGE." How lucky had a man the right to be?

Delennis led off and fanned, but Mel Wessler hit his twenty-fourth homer over the right-field wall. Frohme singled, and then Gilbeau tripled and another New York pitcher was brought in.

Sure, they paid top infielders thirty thousand dollars a year. A guy could keep a family on that and see that the place on West Lancey Street was kept alive. One thing he had to do—write to Dan Kelso right away and be sure of one thing.

The New York catcher ran over to the Philly dugout for a high foul off Stu Avery's bat and tumbled into the dugout. Wyrosnik and Rosch helped him up, and the Quaker trainer asked him how he was. The backstop went back behind the plate, and Avery swung at a curve and missed. Ferrill stepped in to hit.

It was one thing that had to be done, and he'd write Kelso as soon as he got to the hotel. The sign would be large enough for all to see when they walked into that clubhouse.

Ferrill fouled two pitches off, then swung at a bad pitch and dribbled it to the box. Johnny went out with the others to hold the New Yorkers down.

It would have big letters, the sign he'd have Kelso order, for the message it would carry was appropriate for the kids on West Lancey.

The Titan lead-off man singled over short. Wick Ferrill walked the next man, and there was activity in Bucky O'Doul's bull pen. The crowd began to stir. The next man up smashed one to Rosch, and Johnny hopped to second to take the throw. He got it, whirled and threw

207

to Mel for the double play. The crowd gave him a hand and settled back, knowing the Quakers were winning this one, and that they'd get into the series.

That sign would say: "YOU HAVE IT TOUGH? REMEMBER—BABE RUTH NEVER HAD A HOME."